Veil of Hope

A KESSLER EFFECT NOVEL
BOOK FIVE

VANNETTA CHAPMAN

Veil of Hope

Copyright © 2024 by Vannetta Chapman

All rights reserved.

Requests for information should be addressed to: VannettaChapman (at) gmail (dot) com

Any Internet addresses (websites, blogs, etc.) and telephone numbers in this book are offered as a resource. They are not intended in any way to be or imply an endorsement by the author, nor does the author vouch for the content of these sites and numbers for the life of this book.

 Note: This novel is a work of fiction. Names, characters, places, and incidents are either products of the author's imagination or used fictitiously. All characters are fictional, and any similarity to people living or dead is purely coincidental.

Cover design: Streetlight Graphics

First printing, 2024

❈ Created with Vellum

DEDICATION

Dedicated to

The firefighting and emergency crews from
Alpine, Marathon, Terlingua,
Marfa, and Jeff Davis County,
and the
Texas A&M Forest Service

PREFACE

I rise
Up from a past that's rooted in pain
I rise
from "Still I Rise," by Maya Angelou

All that we see or seem
is but a dream within a dream.
from "A Dream Within a Dream,"
by Edgar Allan Poe

CHAPTER 1

J une 6
   The day the lower orbital satellite array began to show signs of instability

GUS MARTINEZ RECEIVED an official text alert at two twenty in the morning of June 4th. It was short on details.

> Time of departure: 04:30. Location: Andrews AFB, Runway 18

That was it. That was all they gave him. Gus wasn't aware of any scheduled exercises. He wasn't even technically in the military. He was a contractor, and he'd never been tapped for war games, combat drills, or training maneuvers. Furthermore, why was he reporting to an Air Force base? He was assigned to McNair. His contract was with the US Army.

Which was not the job he'd envisioned when he earned his PhD in sociology from Stanford. He wasn't sure what he'd expected. His options had been academia or private sector research. Neither appealed to him. Then Uncle Sam came calling. The pay was right, allowing him to knock down his massive student loans. Eleven years later, he still lived in a small apartment in DC and still reported to McNair every day.

He rolled out of bed, padded to the kitchen, pulled a protein bar from the pantry, slipped his to-go mug under the coffee maker, pushed the start button, and hit the shower. Fourteen minutes later, he was ready. As he walked out of his apartment, he turned and glanced back. A stranger would never guess he'd lived there for over a decade. He'd done nothing to personalize it. He told himself twelve-hour days and long working weekends were the price of success in DC. Shaking his head, he vowed that would change. He needed balance in his life—even if he had no idea how to achieve it.

Within twenty-five minutes of receiving the orders, he was on the Suitland Parkway, his go-bag resting on the passenger seat. He was surprised at the amount of DC traffic, given that it was three in the morning. Then, as he was about to take his exit, he heard an explosion to the northeast. At least he thought it was an explosion. His heart rate kicked up a notch, and his palms began to sweat.

When he turned off the Parkway and onto N. Perimeter Road, he came to a sudden and abrupt stop. The backup stretched for over a mile. What was going on? Had the entire base been called up for this exercise?

He picked up his cell and thumbed through various newsfeeds as he inched his way toward the security checkpoint. No headlines regarding the explosion he'd heard. In fact, nothing on the news sites stood out. A blip in the overseas markets. US stock futures were down. Skirmishes in the Middle East. Protests on the West Coast. His social media feeds—where he lurked rather than posted—showed the regular diet of cat memes, political rants, and vacation pictures.

Nothing to indicate there was cause for concern.

No significant news stories.

As he pulled up to the gate, a burly man wearing a United States Army Military Police Corps uniform stepped forward. His name tag said Jones.

"I'll need your ID and pop the trunk for us."

"Seriously?"

"Yup."

Gus gave the man his ID and popped the trunk. He'd been in DC for eleven years. Had been on this particular base a dozen times and McNair hundreds. He knew his face was in the database and his ID would trip the Green Secure Pass indicator on the MP's handheld monitor. He was usually through the gate after a five-second scan of his identification. They hadn't asked to search his trunk since the first day he arrived, fresh from Stanford.

As one MP checked his trunk, another shone a light into his back and front seats, while a third ran an inspection mirror under the car's carriage.

Jones stepped to his window and returned Gus's ID.

"Any idea what's going on?"

"I know even less than you do, man."

"Not sure how that would be possible." Gus drove toward the airstrip, then had to circle the parking area three times looking for a spot. He didn't find one. He finally ended up parking on the grass in a No Parking zone. His choice was to be late or risk a ticket.

He'd take the ticket. The man he reported to, Colonel Dalton Webb, was very keen on punctuality. Gus hadn't spent eleven years working to impress the Colonel only to be busted for being late to a drill.

And if this wasn't a drill? The explosion could have been a terrorist attacking a DC target. A foreign power might be bombarding their eastern ports at this very minute. A dozen possibilities passed through his mind, and he quickly rejected each one. What was happening did not make sense.

Snatching his go-bag off the passenger seat, he jogged toward Runway 18. As he drew closer, he became aware that the place was lit up like it was midday. He stopped abruptly, staring at the sight in front of him. As far down the runway as he could see, aircraft sat nose to tail, engines idling. What was even more curious was that they seemed to be using every type of transport they could get their hands on. A C-130 Hercules was followed by a C-17 Globemaster, which was followed by a C-5M Super Galaxy.

Eleven years ago, he wouldn't have known the names of those aircraft, let alone how many men they were capable of transporting. Short answer to that particular question was a lot. Given the number of planes on the tarmac, he would guess this exercise involved thousands rather than hundreds.

Colonel Webb was easy enough to spot. The man had to be close to six feet, ten inches. He was thin, fit, and almost painfully serious. He cut quite the figure in the glare of floodlights. He stood a few feet from the stairs leading to the closest transport. Beside him was yet another MP, who appeared to be checking IDs—again. The US military's tendency toward paranoia was something Gus had considered writing a paper about, though they'd never let him publish it.

Jogging toward the line that stretched out behind Colonel Webb, he pulled out his ID, accepting the fact that they were playing this one by the book.

"Not that one," the enlisted man in front of him said. He nodded toward Gus's ID pouch. "The other one."

The other one.

Sweat trickled down his neck as he tried to remember the last time he'd seen the damn thing. Someone had shown up at his office one day, switching the old card out with a new one. No explanation. No reason given. No directions as to what it was to be used for. When Gus had asked, the spook—and Gus was sure the guy was from the CIA—had said nonchalantly, "You'll know what it's for when and if the time comes."

Gus had shrugged and stuck it in his ID pouch. Now he fished it out and stared at it. A rather plain, laminated plastic card, with a picture of his face overlaid by gold threads and a string of small numbers across the bottom. No writing. Nothing to indicate its purpose. Nothing on the back.

He moved forward.

Yet another MP held a large black canvas bag, which they were apparently supposed to drop their cell phones into. Gus did so because he worked for the Army, which largely consisted of doing what the guy in front of you did. As he approached the final MP, Webb was called away. Gus held out the mysterious ID.

His heart gave a lurch as the device the MP used to scan the cards emitted a red light. The MP—Murray, according to the name sewn across her uniform—tapped the scanner with the back of her hand—once, twice, then a more emphatic third time.

"Let's try that again."

This time the device emitted a small beep and the light glowed green. Murray met his gaze, and Gus understood in that moment that she didn't know what was going on either. Did anyone? She jerked her head toward the stairs, and he jogged up them, then moved down the aisle of the plane until he found an empty seat on the nearly full aircraft. He stored his bag, dropped into a seat and fastened his seatbelt as the plane began to taxi at a surprising speed.

Had the pilot even said they were lifting off?

And where the hell were they going?

The plane made a rather steep ascent, then turned north and west. North and west. Gus peered out the window, watched the lights of DC fall away as they gained elevation. And that was when all that he'd seen and what little he'd heard came together in his mind. The pieces literally clicked into place.

They were headed to Site R.

They were going to Raven Rock.

He made eye contact with the people he knew—though he didn't know them well. He hadn't exactly made the time to develop lifelong friendships, but you didn't work in a place for over a decade and not learn a few names. They simply shrugged. Most of the faces on the plane, the ones he could see anyway, were not familiar to him. The majority were in their Army combat uniforms, but there were a handful of contractors sprinkled in as well. Gus couldn't come up with a reason for the assorted group of men and women around him, so he checked that question as unanswered and moved on.

If they were headed to Site R, it would be a short flight. The infamous Raven Rock was located less than a hundred miles to the northwest. Situated in Pennsylvania, near the Maryland border, it had been conceived and built during the Cold War. Its purpose? COG, pure and simple. Continuity of government. The threats the US faced might have changed in the last sixty years—more cyber, less nuclear—but the need for a secure command center remained.

The question that Gus was left with was whether this was a drill or the real thing. He closed his eyes and let his mind review what he knew so far. Cryptic text at two twenty in the morning, more traffic flow than usual in DC, an explosion to the northeast, increased security measures at both the gate and the plane, the requirement to show his other identification. A massive number of planes and people. Were they all going to Raven Rock? What percentage of active and reserve service personnel normally deployed for an exercise?

His thoughts froze, and he scrolled them backward like an old 35mm film reel. Why had they kept his phone? He opened his eyes, let his gaze drift forward, left, pretended to pop his neck, and glanced behind him. Identified two men and one woman who were also contractors, plus himself. What did the four of them have in common?

He couldn't get it.

Ken Murphy held a doctorate in economics.

Paul Walker's field was logistics.

Roslynn Green had a PhD in urban planning.

Like Gus, they had all been pursued by Ivy League Universities and Fortune 500 corporations. During the few mixers they'd attended together, he'd learned that, like his offer, theirs had included a better compensation and benefits package than that offered by private industry. Plus, the assurance that what they were doing would make a difference. In his case, the compensation had been almost double what he'd been offered elsewhere. He'd always heard government pay was terrible, but his experience had been the opposite. Uncle Sam was willing to pay for what he needed and wanted.

That was as much as he'd been able to learn from his co-workers, though. Each held a high security clearance, and no one talked about their work. So why were they now all on the same plane, heading toward the government's most notorious underground bunker? The answer was like a smudge on the windshield of a car—there, but only visible enough to be an irritation.

Why had they been instructed to turn over their personal phones? What were phones used for? To call home. Okay. Someone didn't want them calling home. Didn't want them alerting anyone, though at this point they had no information to alert them to.

His thoughts drifted back to a study Colonel Webb had assigned to him three years earlier. Any real deployment to Raven Rock had several problems in their technological age—problems that hadn't existed or been planned for in 1951 when the underground communications center was first conceived. The world had become one big petri dish that sat under the microscope of the populace.

Everyone knew everything about everyone else.

Even early drills in the 1950s showed people from all levels of the military refusing to go if their families weren't included. Of course, that had been during the Cold War. No one was keen on leaving their family to be vaporized by a nuclear bomb while they sheltered in a bunker. Then there was the issue of keeping a massive COG deployment secret long enough for the tapped officials to be whisked away. How did you avoid massive panic in a society that lived perpetually on the edge of the next disaster?

If those going alerted those who weren't...

If those with IDs alerted those without...

There would be chaos—in the military and the government. There would be pandemonium in the streets. Gus's report had concluded that even if such a movement were only a drill, the societal repercussions would be far-reaching and irreversible. Smaller exercises, of course, continued. Sometimes select news personnel were invited to tag along. Best to get ahead of the breaking news stories. But a large scale exercise like what he was seeing today? Nope. Wouldn't happen. Probably couldn't happen. Unless it wasn't an exercise.

His thoughts skittered back to the cell phones. Mobile devices weren't only used to communicate. They were also used to gather information. What had he read on his phone?

A downturn in overseas trading—so whatever was happening was global. US futures were down—indicating some traders on Wall Street already knew about it. Skirmishes in the Middle East were too common to draw any conclusions from, as were protests on the West Coast. They'd become a land of wars and rumors of wars, protesting anything and everything they didn't understand.

Then he thought of something his pop had once said. "Society hangs by a thread, son. Thread can be strong, like spider web silk. Strong as steel."

Gus hadn't believed that. He'd done a web search later that night, and of course, his old man had been right.

"It's not indestructible though—strong winds, heavy rain, even contact with a small animal can cause it to snap. Our modern society is like that. It's strong, but it could so easily snap."

Was that what had happened?

Had the string that held their society together snapped?

And then, just as the plane began its descent, Gus's mind formed another connection. Johnson. Walker. Green. Himself. Even the Colonel. They all had one thing in common—they were effectively alone in the world.

Divorced or never married. No children.

No siblings.

Parents deceased.

He certainly had no one he felt an urgent need to call and warn that the world as they knew it might be ending. His mother had died several years earlier from cancer. His pop not long after that from a massive heart attack. He had no siblings. No spouse or children.

And that was when he knew with complete certainty that this was not merely a drill.

~

THEY LANDED at Thurmont Airstrip in Maryland and were loaded into transport trucks. Gus knew immediately he wasn't the only one who had figured out what was happening.

"Think it's the real thing?" Ken asked.

"If it's not, they're doing a fine job of faking it." Roslynn sat forward, elbows on her knees, fingers interlaced together. She was the only one of the group of four contractors who might have passed for military—muscular, tough, intense dark eyes, and long black hair pulled into a severe bun. Everything about Roslynn screamed she was not to be messed with. "I've never participated in a drill. Have you?"

Gus, Ken, and Paul all shook their heads.

"Most likely scenario?" Gus asked.

Paul, their logistics expert, took that one. He was the oldest and had been contracting with the US military the longest. It showed, too—he was balding, had something of a paunch, and looked like he hadn't seen the sun in quite some time. "Something to do with tech. Something that probably resulted in a major breach of security."

"Enough of a breach to rattle Dalton Webb." Ken ran his fingers through his red, spiked hair. The youngest of their group, he was thin to the point of appearing gaunt. Tattoos covered most visible skin, including his neck and the backs of his hands, and he wore a pair of designer glasses.

They'd all four recently gathered for drinks to celebrate Ken's 25th birthday at the Dacha Beer Garden in DC. Like the few other times they'd met for drinks, it had ended early with everyone claiming they still had more work to do.

"Heard him talking to someone as he walked away from the landing strip," Ken said. "Webb's usually curt, but this went way beyond that. Whatever has happened, it's something he hasn't dealt with before, maybe hasn't even considered."

"I doubt there's anything Colonel Webb hasn't considered," Paul argued. "But you're correct in your assessment. Something unnerved him."

At the speed the transport was going, they would make quick work of the twelve miles to the Raven Rock Mountain Complex. Gus tried to recall everything he'd learned in his study of the RRMC. It had been upgraded over the years to better accommodate changes in technology, but the facility itself hadn't undergone much of a change. It basically looked the same as it did in the 2013 science fiction movie *Oblivion*.

Or, as Ken so aptly pointed out, "I feel like I'm headed inside *Fallout*."

Gus had forgotten he was a gamer. Ken might know more about the facility than he did. By all accounts, the video game had been eerily accurate. Still, the group turned to Gus as they approached the site.

"Tell us about it," Roslynn said, lowering her voice to a whisper, not that anyone could hear them over the rattle of the truck and the many conversations going on between different groups in the back of the transport.

"Beyond what you've seen of it in pop culture?"

"Pretend I don't know anything about pop culture."

Roslynn was serious, but Gus couldn't help smiling. Roslynn had no online presence, distrusted most technology, and still carried a flip phone. For an urban planner, she was oddly out of sync with the current times.

"OK. The land was seized by the government in January of '51 and work on the facility began immediately. Three underground buildings were completed by '53. Originally it was designed to provide an alternate site for the Pentagon. The complex itself is built into the mountain to take advantage of the granite structure as a shield."

"From nukes?" Ken pushed up his glasses.

"From anything," Paul answered, then he motioned for Gus to go on.

"Multiple underground levels, extensive tunnels, living quarters to accommodate a lot of people."

"A lot?" Ken shook his head. "Can you be more specific?"

"Nope. Specific details aren't normally released. I'd put the number north of fifteen thousand. I was tasked with doing a sociological study of how people within and without would respond to a lengthy stay."

"Lengthy?" Ken looked nervous. "How lengthy? Months?"

Gus shook his head. "Years."

And then they were there, and conversations, including theirs, stopped. As they stepped out of the transport, they saw work crews installing a fenced barrier around the complex, complete with concertina wire at the top. Patrolling behind the work crews were soldiers holding M26 shotguns at the ready.

Definitely not a drill.

Gus didn't consider himself a claustrophobic, but neither did he particularly like the idea of taking shelter inside a mountain. He might have thought twice about stepping into an underground bunker if he'd been given even a few seconds to mull over his options upon their approach. He wasn't. They lined up with the others and jogged toward the entrance. Maybe the idea of being locked out was worse than the idea of being locked in.

When they were mere feet from the entrance, shots rang out behind them—from the direction of the street. Gus turned, craned his neck to see what was happening. He thought the initial shots came from the other side of the fence, and it was immediately met with a barrage of fire from the soldiers keeping watch over the workers.

Several people screamed.

A woman began to wail.

Another person barked an order.

And before they could understand what had happened, or why, they were hurried inside, through the massive steel and concrete doors designed to withstand a nuclear blast. Hustling down an incredibly long corridor with fluorescent lights, Gus noticed that they passed three times through similarly constructed doorways—redundancy in case an outer entrance was breached.

He knew from his research that Raven Rock resembled a city, complete with fire department, police department, medical facilities, dining hall, and sleeping quarters. It wasn't the only such facility. COG facilities also included Cheyenne Mountain Complex near Colorado Springs, Mount Weather in Virginia, and Yucca Mountain in West Virginia—which was purportedly closed down years earlier, though his cursory research had indicated that might not be the case.

He'd also come across numerous and persistent rumors that other secret facilities might exist. Black ops. Off budget. Spread across the United States. Even he couldn't guess at how many in total.

The long corridor dumped them into a massive room. At the end of it was a makeshift platform with a podium, microphone, and several three and four-star generals. Gus, Ken, Paul, and Roslynn fell into formation with the men and women serving under Dalton Webb. No one spoke. The time for idle chatter was past. As the enormous room filled, Gus realized that this was his Rubicon—a dividing point in his life, a decision that could not be reversed. After today, his memories, assuming he lived long enough to look back on this time, would be divided into before stepping into Site R and after.

When it seemed the room could hold no more, General Kendricks stepped to the podium. He wore an Army combat uniform. Four stars adorned the center of his cap as well as the shoulders of his uniform. He looked to be in his sixties. His expression was grave, his eyes—even from a distance—piercing.

"As you have no doubt surmised, this is not a drill. At seven minutes past zero one hundred hours, US Strategic Command was notified that a cataclysmic collision of our lower orbital satellite system is imminent. This facility, like others around the country, was activated and is now fully staffed. We will remain in this site until we have received the all-clear. It is imperative that you perform your duties as assigned and perform them well. The fate of this nation, of our country, could very well depend on it."

And then he dismissed them. Within each division, they were given directions as to where they would bunk, as well as when and where they would report for duty. Gus, Ken, Paul, and Roslynn stood frozen in place, uncertain if they were supposed to find their bunks or report to someone and receive their duty assignments. They didn't have to wonder for long. They were approached by a major whose nametag said Lawrence. "The Colonel wants a word."

"With me?" Gus said, feeling ridiculous when his voice came out in a high pitch resembling an elementary student.

"All of you."

Kendricks turned away. Gus and his group of compatriots exchanged a look, then hurried to catch up. They were led out of the cavernous room and down another long corridor, where Kendricks stopped at a door that looked like all the others save for the number 1083. Kendricks knocked once, waited for

Webb's command to enter, then opened the door. He didn't join them, but something in his gaze said *good luck.*

Colonel Webb sat on one side of a metal, WWII-style desk and nodded toward the four empty chairs across from him. As one, they sat.

"You four are in a unique position to provide information that our government needs." He pushed four additional nametags toward them. Like the mysterious badge that had allowed Gus to board the plane, this had his photo on the front, overlaid with stripes—appropriately colored red, white, and blue. But instead of numbers, at the bottom, there were the letters KESLRFTF.

Paul tapped the letters and arched his eyebrows.

"You are now members of the Kessler Effect Short and Long-Range Forecast Task Force."

As one, they raised their gaze from the ID cards to Webb, but it was Roslynn who voiced their disbelief. "The Kessler Effect? It's happened?"

"Is happening, as we speak, and will continue to happen over the next few days."

"How widespread?" Ken asked.

"Global."

"Percentage of satellites affected?" Ken leaned forward. "It can't be all of them."

Webb's scowl grew even more pronounced. "At this point, we are assuming the worst-case scenario, which unfortunately seems to be the direction we're headed."

"Inciting incident?" Gus asked. It would make a difference. If this was started by a foreign entity, the American people— hell, the entire world—would be out for blood. If it was a natural event, if that could be proven, it might at least mitigate the hostilities between nations.

"Undetermined. You three will bunk together." Webb

inclined his head toward Green. "We have you in a female barracks down the hall."

"I'd rather be with my team, Sir."

Webb considered her for a moment, then nodded. "Thought you might say that. There are two desks and four beds in the room you're sharing. You'll have to make the best of it. I've already instructed Major Lawrence to see that you are each issued air-gapped laptops. They'll connect to the private network here in RRMC. I want a short-term analysis from each of you in your specific field on my desk by thirteen hundred hours and a long-term one by fifteen hundred hours tomorrow. That's all."

Once again dismissed, they filed out of the office. Lawrence led them down another long hall, nodded at the room they were to bunk in but didn't slow, made three more turns and stopped in front of a supply window. Their newest IDs were checked, and they were each handed an HP EliteBook 840 G6 Rugged. These people weren't messing around. They were sequestered inside a mountain, and still the laptops were outfitted to withstand an EMP.

"The biometrics are set so that only you can use and operate your device," the technician explained.

Lawrence dumped them in the mess hall after confirming they could find their way back to their office/lodging.

"I'm actually not sure I can," Ken admitted after the major had walked away. "This is a lot to process, and I'm not good with directions in the best of times."

"Stick with us, kid." Roslynn dug into the chow.

Gus thought the blob on his plate looked like some combination of lasagna and meatloaf. Regardless, he wolfed it down. He hadn't eaten a thing since the protein bar he'd absentmindedly consumed while driving toward Andrews AFB. He'd finished the last of it and the coffee just before he'd seen the explosion. Had that been the first satellite to fall? Or something that exploded because the computerized safety systems no longer worked?

How many other explosions had there been since the first?

How many people killed?

He might have become completely immobilized by the number and direction of his questions, but his group pulled his attention back to the present—their present—situation.

"We have four hours to get Webb those short-term reports," Ken said around a mouthful of lasagna goo.

"Start with what we know." Paul pointed his fork toward the ceiling, actually toward the mountain above them. "David Kessler predicted that a cataclysmic collision of satellites was inevitable due to the sheer number of devices and amount of space debris rotating the earth at or below twelve hundred miles."

"The sky above us resembles an overcrowded DC highway." Roslynn scraped the last bite from her plate, savored it, then dropped the fork. "Kessler went on to posit that once such an event began, it would be impossible to stop."

Gus pushed aside his empty plate and crossed his arms on the table. "I checked my newsfeeds before we had to give up our phones. Blip in overseas trading and US futures were down—nothing to indicate an event of this magnitude."

"Why hasn't trading been halted?" Ken took off his glasses, cleaned them with his shirttail, and pushed them back into place. "That's literally what the circuit breakers are for."

"If they halt trading, they tip off John and Jane Doe to the magnitude of what is happening. They can't afford to do that. Not until the Continuity of Government plans are in place—nationally and globally." Roslynn tapped her fingers against the table. "Anyone have people out there?"

Ken, Paul, and then Gus all shook their heads.

"Neither do I, which I suspect is why we were chosen."

"Well, it could be because we're the brightest," Gus argued.

"Yeah. And Santa could come down the chimney tonight, but I doubt it." Roslynn steepled her fingers together. "Not only that, but redundancy is a big thing in the US military."

"Meaning?" Ken asked.

"Meaning that there are other groups like us at other facilities. They'll compare our reports, see if they line up."

Paul stood and stretched. "Better get to work then."

None of them suggested that retreating to the bunker was an overreaction. They might have specialized in different fields, but they tacitly agreed with the primary conclusion that Uncle Sam had reached. The results of yanking technology from a country almost completely dependent on it would be far-reaching and catastrophic.

The room they were to bunk in was the size of a closet—literally. There were two bunk beds—one on each side of the door—and two desks—opposite the door. A cat could have circled the room without ever touching the floor. Paul and Ken took the desks. Roslynn spread out on a top bunk, and Gus took the opposite bottom bunk.

They spent the next three and a half hours lost in their work. The laptops were quick and powerful and though they weren't connected to the World Wide Web, Gus was able to find everything he needed within the government database. No one in the small room shared their conclusions. They didn't have to because each person on the team was fairly certain on what they'd find and that it would reflect what the others discovered. The situation was worse than even Dr. Donald J. Kessler had posited in 1978. Of course, the amount of satellites and debris had increased exponentially since then. And the degree to which society depended on those devices had also increased. The result was that Gus's research and his report both developed pretty much as he had thought they would from the minute that Colonel Webb had said the word Kessler.

He knew with unsettling certainty that they wouldn't be leaving Site R anytime in the near future.

For better or worse, they were locked inside a mountain.

CHAPTER 2

Colonel Webb looked worse than he had just four hours earlier. His face was pale, his eyes blinked rapidly, and he had a slight tremor in his right hand. Surprisingly, he began by updating them on the status of things.

"As you may or may not be aware, The White House Army Signal Corps maintains permanent detachments at Raven Rock, Mount Weather, and Camp David. I can now confirm that all critical level government officials—save one—are sequestered in one of those facilities."

Gus squirmed in his seat.

Save one?

Which one? If it was the Speaker of the House, it might not matter. If it was the President, it most certainly did.

"Mount Weather will be primarily focused on military and overseas missions with the State Department—though the extent to which we can remain in contact with anyone off-continent remains to be seen. Raven Rock will be primarily concerned with restoring domestic operations. While there are analysts like yourselves at Mount Weather, they were included for purposes of redundancy as well as to confirm or contradict your projections. To summarize, your work will be to predict and plan for domestic situations."

Purposes of redundancy, as Roslynn had suggested.

But why the double attention to domestic matters?

Mount Weather had a massive above-ground complex as well as nearly 700,000 square feet below ground. Did they think Mount Weather could be breached? Did they consider that team to be at risk? Or were they at risk inside Raven Rock? Perhaps it was neither of those things. Perhaps it was the military being, as was its custom, paranoid.

"Up until today, you have worked largely in isolation from one another. Beginning today, I expect you to coordinate your findings and use one another's conclusions to inform your work going forward. To that end, Murphy, brief us on what you found."

Ken straightened his shoulders and pulled in a deep breath. Though he was the youngest of the group, he was usually quite cocky. At the moment, he seemed everything but that. His eyes flitted from one spot to another, he repeatedly ran the fingertips of his right hand over the tats on his left wrist, and his right leg bounced as if he were keeping time to a grunge beat. "The current economic system as we know it will not survive a total collapse of the lower orbital satellite grid."

Ken paused and Webb glowered at him. Finally, the Colonel said, "Explain."

"The vast majority of workers are paid through bank transfers, and those transfers will stop when the internet ceases to be accessible. Workers will stop going to work—whether because the transit system no longer works, the gas pumps go empty, or they aren't getting paid—and the entire supply chain will break down. Money will become worthless because there's nothing on the shelf to purchase. When that happens—"

"Your conclusions are worthless unless you can be more specific," Webb growled.

"My research indicates a complete economic breakdown will occur within twenty-four to forty-eight hours of the inciting event. Within hours of that, anarchy will ensue."

"Literally?" Webb asked.

"Yes. One man's private property becomes another man's —Walmart. Furthermore, agriculture, mining, and forestry will immediately come to a halt."

Webb wiped away a bead of sweat from his forehead. "Explain the agriculture to me."

"Seventy percent of large farms use the Global Positioning System for precision farming, remote sensing technology to monitor crop conditions, even automatic feeders and automatic milking systems for cows. We don't have enough people who know how or would be willing to go back to the pre-technological way of doing things."

"This all happens in the short-term?" Webb confirmed.

"Yes, sir."

It was obvious to Gus that the colonel was not happy with the answers he was receiving.

Webb snapped, "Anything else?"

"Domestic and international trade will quickly come to a halt. The people in Florida will be stuck with a lot of oranges and those in Texas will have cotton—which, last I checked, you cannot eat."

Webb straightened a folder on his desk so that it was perfectly perpendicular to the desk's edge. He let his gaze drift over each of them, then nodded at Paul Walker.

Paul wasn't nervous. Being the oldest in the group, he'd no doubt been through stressful situations before. Nothing like this though. His entire demeanor seemed somewhat deflated.

"As Ken just outlined, the supply and demand chain will break down almost immediately. Seventy percent or more of inventory control is done through automation. If you're talking about e-commerce businesses like Amazon, that number is closer to ninety-five percent."

"Goods don't simply disappear from warehouses because the internet is down," Webb said.

"True, but once the grid fails, which it will, there's no way for a warehouse to know what items need to be shipped to which location."

"What else?"

"Transportation such as subways and commuter trains will fail immediately. They're all dependent on GPS for speed, coordination with other like transportation, and scheduling." Paul stared at his hands for a moment, opening them as if a better answer might be written on his palms. Shaking his head, he continued, "A cursory study has convinced me that the most detrimental of changes will be the complete lack of information. We, as a nation, have become addicted to it and when you take that away—when you take away communication—the result will be mass chaos."

Webb's nod was curt, his face emotionless. He barked, "Green."

Roslynn's posture remained ramrod straight, her gaze unflinching, but Gus noticed a tic beneath her right eye. They'd been in this less than twenty-four hours and already they were all showing physical signs of the strain. His gut felt like he'd been on an all-night bender, and his hands wouldn't stop sweating.

"Urban areas will feel the effect more quickly than rural, but without a doubt it will affect everyone—or 99 percent of everyone." Roslynn plunged ahead, not waiting for Webb to grill her with questions. "A few remote towns, independent ranchers, and survivalists might not be aware immediately, but eventually, even those people drive to town for milk and bread. Within the urban circle, much will depend on how long law enforcement stays on the job."

"The National Guard has already been deployed."

"To where?" Gus asked.

"Everywhere."

Gus was already shaking his head. Just because they were called up didn't mean they would go. Some would. Some wouldn't. It would be a bandage at best. He didn't voice any of this, because Roslynn was still talking.

"Some local governments will fare better than others, but once utilities and basic services stop, city councils are bound to fall apart too."

"Which basic services?"

"All of them. People need water and sewage. The release of water to municipalities is controlled by computer programs. Local water supplies will deplete within twenty-four hours. Trash will stack up on the curb. Sewage will back up in homes. Police will, almost inevitably, not be able to keep up with calls for help. Doctors and nurses won't be able to get to work and even if they could, a great amount of medical care is also dependent on technology."

"Such as?"

"Such as prescriptions at a hospital. There's not a pharmacist standing in front of shelves of medicine. There's a machine that dispenses what's needed when an authorized person enters a code."

"Who fills up the machine?" Webb ran a finger over his right eyebrow. "Never mind. Walker and Murphy have already answered that. A computer alerts a warehouse to what is needed, the medications are loaded on a truck, and a delivery person takes them to the hospital. Only the computer won't work and the delivery person won't be able to make it from the warehouse to the hospital."

He turned his gaze to Gus.

"I wish I had better news," Gus said.

"I don't need better news, Martinez. I want to know what's happening out there right now and what we can expect to happen in the next forty-eight hours."

So much for trying to ease the colonel's concern.

Gus crossed his arms and gave it to him straight. "Sociologically, we're a country of individuals that highly value our privacy but are completely dependent on one another for the most basic of things. Which is to say, we may know the name of our Amazon delivery person, but we rarely know the name of our neighbor."

His thoughts flashed back to his apartment—a place where he slept, showered, and ate standing up at the counter. It was hardly a home. He couldn't name one other resident in his apartment building. Then he thought of his father's prediction that the thread that held society together could so easily break.

Clearing his throat, he focused on the report he was delivering. "Fifty percent of people will make an attempt to work together for the first twelve to twenty-four hours, until they realize that help isn't coming. Then it will be each man for himself."

"The other fifty percent?" Webb held his gaze. "What will they be doing right now?"

Instead of answering that question, Gus said, "Survivalists once operated under the concept of *seventy-two hours to animal.* The foundational idea of that term being that the success of emergency preparedness and disaster response depended on that first seventy-two hours after a catastrophic event. As evidenced in our response to the global pandemic, people tend to panic more quickly than that. The run on toilet paper within the first twenty-four hours is an innocuous example. We no longer trust one another and politically we are polarized. Add to that our ever-increasing dependence on technology, and *seventy-two hours to animal* has trended down until some now say it's more like seventy-two minutes."

"Which has passed," Paul said.

"Yeah."

Webb, for once, answered candidly. "It won't help that we have planes falling out of the sky."

"What?" Ken sat forward, his body tense as if he were in full flight-or-fight mode. Was that what he'd heard driving into Andrews AFB?

"Additionally, one of those incidents was recorded on X, formerly known as Twitter, before that site went down." Webb pressed his fingertips to his forehead. "Our executive branch made the decision to deactivate the stock market's circuit breakers—hoping to buy a little time, which it did. However, now the market is in a spiral and you can be sure that every retired bloke with an online trading account knew what happened as soon as the markets opened."

"That doesn't sound good," Roslynn said.

"The Dow dropped eighty percent before it went offline. All news stations are also down. In fact, everything is offline. The internet, as we've come to know it, no longer exists."

Gus tried to envision that, tried to conceive all of the ways that would affect everyday life—which was exactly what he'd done in his report to Webb. Only this was different. This wasn't hypothetical. It was happening, and it felt oddly personal. If he were out there, instead of inside Raven Rock, what would he be facing? What would and wouldn't work?

It was a question he didn't have a chance to ask because a

blaring alarm sounded at the same moment that an emergency light began to flash red. Webb jumped to his feet and rushed out the door before Gus could process what was happening. He heard the words "Follow me," and looked at Paul, Roslynn, and Ken.

All stood and gazed around as if the answer might be written on the walls. Then—largely because they worked for the Army—they did as they were told, rushing down the corridors, attempting to keep up with Colonel Dalton Webb, and wondering what else could have possibly gone wrong.

THEY CAUGHT up with Webb outside another massive steel door. The alarm echoing off the concrete walls made Gus's ears ring, and the continuous red flashing light caused his pulse to race. They'd passed plenty of soldiers who seemed to know where to go during a literal red alert. All were jogging, eyes focused straight ahead, expressions betraying nothing.

Instead of flashing his ID in front of the reader next to the door, Webb stepped closer and stood perfectly still while a security device performed an eye scan. There was a click, the deadbolt slid free, and he opened the door. He glanced back once to make sure they were still with him.

Gus, Ken, Paul, and Roslynn stepped into the room and froze. It wasn't that the scene was chaotic. Order reigned in spite of the blaring alarm. The surprising thing was that the room was filled with computer terminals. Dozens of display screens covered every inch of three walls. The place reminded Gus of NASA's control center.

Each computer station was manned and most had at least one general or colonel standing behind them. All of that was to be expected. It was what was on the screens that Gus couldn't believe. He'd just predicted as much to Webb, but that was different. That was theoretical. That hadn't happened.

And yet now it had.

His eyes drifted to the screen front and center, which showed a mass of people climbing over the fence that surrounded the White House. They'd breached the gate as well, and instead of firing, the soldiers fell back. Whether that was out of concern for their fellow man or because they'd been ordered to do so, Gus didn't know.

Then the mass of humanity was covering the lawn, surging toward the President's residence. Here, too, the guards had retreated.

"There's no one there," Webb muttered. "All they're going to find is empty rooms and a few artifacts."

The screens fanning to the left of center showed similar scenes in Chicago, Dallas, New York, and Los Angeles. One of the screens to the right looked like something Gus had once seen when he'd toured an air traffic control center. Lines arched over the United States in a dozen different directions. General Kendricks moved behind the young man monitoring the flight trajectories. "How many?"

"Currently three thousand, eight hundred and twenty-two, Sir."

"How many have we lost?"

"Eighty-one."

"Cause?"

"A few were mid-air collisions. Others were hit by falling satellite debris." The soldier's voice shook, but she kept her attention on the screen and continued to do her job.

Gus could not imagine how much resolve that must require.

"Some simply disappeared, Sir. No data sent."

"All of this is disturbing," Paul muttered. "But none of it explains the alarm."

As if hearing him, Kendricks barked at a lieutenant to shift what was on his screen to the main one, and then Gus understood the alarm. A large group of people had attempted to breach the perimeter fence of Raven Rock. It was surreal to look at that picture and realize he was looking at the mountain and the bunker beneath it. He was looking at the very place where he was standing.

In this case, the guards did not fall back.

A colonel wearing ACUs stood in the open bed of a supply truck. He raised a bull horn to his lips, and General Kendricks said in an even voice, "Let us hear the audio."

"You need to move back from the perimeter fence. This is your last warning."

Instead of complying, someone in the front of the mass of people pulled a gun. A soldier on the inside of the fence aimed and fired before the man could get off a shot. As he crumpled to the ground, the colonel signaled to someone behind him and men carrying large hoses pushed forward as guards moved back. The hoses looked like what a firefighter might use, and then the power was cranked up and a massive, powerful stream of water was directed toward the protestors. Men and women fell to the ground as others attempted to drag them away. The violence of the water seemed to affect them more than the injury of the man who had pulled the gun. He, too, was carried away and within sixty seconds, the protestors had backed off and regrouped thirty yards from the fence.

Gus had done a brief report on the use of water cannons to disperse crowds. He understood their purpose was to create a physical barrier between rioters and law enforcement. Though they were a nonlethal form of crowd control, they could sometimes escalate tensions rather than reduce it. Also, they'd only work as long as there was available water pressure. How much water did Raven Rock have? And how much were they willing to spend on maintaining a perimeter?

Kendricks picked up a phone and was apparently patched in to the colonel leading the defense. On the screen, the man pulled out a large satellite phone and held it to his ear.

Kendricks said, "Pull back the water cannons, and I want the electricity turned on to that fence now. Double the amount of guards. By the time the sun sets, I want tactical lights illuminating every inch of ground that surrounds this site."

He slammed the receiver down, was called to another terminal, and stormed through a door at the side of the room.

Webb turned to them and jerked his head toward the hall. When they'd all trooped after him and the massive door had shut, followed by a click of the lock, he said, "I wanted you to see that. You need to know what's happening in real-time if you stand a chance of predicting what we're going to have to deal with next."

And then he strode away.

Gus, Ken, Paul, and Roslynn stared at one another, then slowly began making their way down the hall. They didn't go back to their room. Gus couldn't imagine going there right now. Why? To sleep? He felt as if he'd never sleep again. And he couldn't do any additional research. What they'd just seen—it confirmed what they'd reported to Webb. He had the bizarre thought that their words had caused it.

As they entered the mess hall, he said, "I need some caffeine."

When Paul gave him a pointed look, Gus spread his hands out as if to say, *What?*

"Water—you need to hydrate. And food—you barely ate half of your lunch. Both will help..." He shook his head, then mumbled, "Help things to settle."

Ken followed him to the food line, which seemed to have a continuous line of soldiers. As they shuffled toward the front, Ken said, "Suspecting something is one thing. Knowing it is another. Seeing it?"

He'd kept his voice low, but the soldier in front of them in the line overheard, turned, and said, "Seeing it messes with your mind."

Which Gus thought pretty much summed it up.

Twenty minutes later the four newest members of the KESLRFTF Task Force still hadn't managed to process what they'd witnessed in the command center. It was Roslynn who sat forward, her hands splayed out on the table, and issued a call to action.

"There isn't a damn thing we can do about what is happening out there right now."

"Your point?" Gus asked. He wasn't being confrontational. He really wanted to know.

"My point is that we need to do our jobs. Just like the soldiers around us are doing their jobs. We continue to analyze. We assess. We get in front of the problems. Instead of just predicting, we come up with ways to help the people who are on the outside. Because if they're acting like what we just saw after less than twenty-four hours..."

"Seventy-two minutes to animal," Ken said. He pushed up his glasses and added, "I've heard of it. I suspect every gamer has heard of it."

"I don't believe it." Paul tapped his fist against the table. "I refuse to believe it. If I did believe it, then we can be sure that there will be nothing to return to once they let us out of this place."

"You're not wrong," Gus said. "It's inevitable that some people will respond with panic, anger, and violence."

Roslynn sat back now, still keeping her voice low. "A pretty bad combination, but not everyone will react that way."

"We could run an analysis on the outliers," Gus said, the answer forming as he tried to articulate it. "Determine what groups will choose to work together. Gather the facts, compute the averages, come up with a list of those most likely to survive."

Roslynn drummed her fingers on the table, the beginnings of a smile tugging at her lips. "Then we provide that list when Webb comes asking."

"Which he will." Ken was sitting up straight now. His expression had changed from surrender to determination.

And Gus felt it too.

They weren't hiding beneath the mountain merely to catalog the end. They were in Raven Rock to help usher in a new beginning.

"It's not what he's asked for, though." Paul held up his hands in surrender. "Don't shoot me for stating the obvious. I agree with what you're all saying. But the point of the matter is that what Webb has asked for is vastly different from what you're describing, and neither set of data will be easy to get. Our long-term analysis is due at fifteen hundred hours tomorrow."

"And once we turn that in, he'll ask for something else." Roslynn sank back. "Paul's right. If we do this, if we try to analyze and project the survivors in this thing, we'll have to do it on our own time."

"Something the US Army isn't great about providing," Paul pointed out.

But Gus still felt that buzz of possibility. The faint and glimmering light of hope. "It'll mean working even longer hours—giving Webb whatever he needs and then pursuing our own project when we should be sleeping."

It was Ken who put that fact in perspective. "It's the only way I'll survive this with my sanity intact. Playing *Fallout* is one thing. Living it is another. Taking refuge inside a mountain while the world falls apart was not on my list of things I ever wanted to do. But if we can do this... If we can come up with what they need before they even know to ask for it, maybe it will be worth it."

Once back in their room, the other three went straight to work—at least Gus thought they were working. He didn't. He needed time to process all that had happened in the last twenty-four hours. He kept thinking about his apartment, how he'd turned and looked at it and understood how bare it was.

How bare his life was.

Why? Why had he sacrificed everything for his career? So he could sit out the global apocalypse in a bunker? He'd rather be out there, with people he cared about and people who cared about him. The problem with that was he'd totally isolated himself from everyone else. Why?

He lay on his back in his bottom bunk, arms behind his head, fingers interlaced, and stared at the bottom of the bunk above him. He understood what he was struggling with—regret. And he also understood that he was in shock. Who wouldn't be?

But the regret was bitter.

It was a rock in the pit of his stomach, and he didn't think it would go away until he stepped out of Raven Rock Mountain Complex and took in a giant lungful of fresh air.

He couldn't know for certain if that would ever happen, but if it did, he wouldn't waste a second chance.

He would choose to live and live fully.

He would do everything differently.

If he got a chance.

CHAPTER 3

The following seven days were the most stressful of Gus's life. The reports of what was happening outside the bunker were horrendous, eclipsing even his worst predictions. Local police lost control in the first twelve hours. The National Guard showed up in some places and set up a perimeter around financial sectors and town squares. But soon the people inside those perimeters realized that they were as trapped as the people on the outside. Apparently, from what they were able to gather inside Raven Rock, the people on the inside insisted on being let out. When the Guard had no one to protect, they attempted to help the local populace.

Very quickly, people figured out that the Guard didn't have food, medicine, or supplies to disperse. The guardsmen and women found themselves on the receiving end of the populace's fear and anger. By day five they withdrew and reorganized.

But the reorganization was piecemeal at best. Although the COG facilities could still communicate with one another due to landlines that had been installed years earlier, commanders weren't able to communicate with their men and women in the field. When leadership evaporated, most units dispersed.

A few, though, found they were under the supervision of someone who had the skills, foresight, and ambition to seize the reins. Those three characteristics, found together and in abundance, did not often belong to model citizens. Roslynn was put in charge of attempting to track these groups. Gus didn't envy her that particular task. Spending twelve hours a day creating dossiers and analytical charts on megalomaniacs while trapped inside an underground bunker wasn't his idea of a choice assignment.

As for their small task force, they ate together, slept together, and worked together. Maybe it was because they weren't actually military personnel, or perhaps it was the nature of the event they were going through, but very quickly they formed a solid, cohesive group. Closer than coworkers or friends, they became like family to one another. And when they were alone, when they were exhausted enough to drop their guard, they expressed their greatest fears to one another.

"What if someone gets hold of the nukes?" Ken jiggled his right leg as they sat in the mess hall. It was three in the morning, and the place had a spattering of people spread throughout the room. With over fifteen thousand people residing in Site R, someone was always eating.

"This bunker was built to withstand just such a scenario," Paul reminded him.

"I get that. We'll survive, but what about everyone out there?"

Every conversation went back to that. What would happen to the people outside the bunker? They'd heard through the grapevine that the president was at Mount Weather and the vice president was at Cheyenne Mountain. They had the illustrious honor of housing the head of the Joint Chiefs. As for the person who was missing, there were any number of rumors—the president's wife, the head of the Federal Reserve, all of the Supreme Court Justices. They were just that—rumors.

Gus wasn't really sure it mattered. The US government would need to be reinvented when this event was over—if it was ever *over*.

"I heard a nuke went off over Chicago," Gus said.

"It's not a rumor." Roslynn had been focused on her MRE, but now she glanced up. "I saw the live video in the control room."

"Where were we?"

Roslynn shrugged. "Asleep, I assume. When I can't sleep, I roam. Kendricks happened by and told me to follow him, which I did. There wasn't a lot to see though..." Her voice trailed off, and she resumed scraping the food out of her MRE package.

Some days their meals were served on plates, like in a school cafeteria. Other days workers set out large containers of MREs. Gus picked what seemed the most palatable and added water—an efficient if tasteless way to consume calories. Each time Gus thought that, and he inevitably did every time he ripped open a pouch and added water, his mind drifted to the people on the outside. He was acutely aware that they'd be happy to have what he was eating.

"A nuke in Chicago?" Paul drummed his fingers against the table. "I can't believe we didn't hear about something that big."

Roslynn shrugged. "One more tragedy in a long line of tragedies. Plus, you three don't get out much."

"And you do?" Gus asked, reaching for the half-eaten MRE she'd lost interest in.

When Roslynn gave him a pointed look, he mouthed,

"Waste not, want not," and she laughed. It wasn't much, but it was something. He worried about Roslynn. Worried about all of them. How long could people survive under this type of pressure? Would they find one of their group at the main steel door, pounding on it and begging to be let out? Or curled up on their bunk, unable to analyze one other horrific thing?

No one complained.

They carried on as if it were any other day at the office.

"Any idea who set it off?" Paul asked. "Was it an accident? An act of war? Terrorism?"

"We don't know," Roslynn's tone was flat, practical, analytical. "Could have been any of those things. With the grid down, the nuclear power plants aren't really under anyone's control. The ones that were shut down per the emergency protocols are probably okay. But not everyone was warned with enough time to do so."

"Any overseas chatter?" Gus asked.

"Very little. From what I've heard—and I didn't receive this information directly or confirm it—the president has been in contact with heads of state throughout the world. Per my source—"

"You have a source?" Ken looked taken aback.

Roslynn stared at him a moment, then reached out and patted him on the head. "You're so cute when you act innocent."

"According to your source..." Gus prompted.

"Every country has their hands full dealing with domestic matters. No one is looking to start a war."

"Though this would be the perfect time," Gus said. "With our defenses down."

"They're not though. Military satellites are still working. We can still see what's going on all over the world, but I'm not sure we're able to coordinate deployments of military personnel. I doubt any country can do that. Communication satellites are still functional, but they don't work well when a debris field exists between the sender and the receiver." Gus was thinking about his most recent assignment from Colonel Webb. Identify, catalog, and analyze what satellites were left in mid and upper orbit. Lower orbit was still a debris field. While the great majority of the satellites had fallen—many burning up as they entered Earth's orbit—some remained in an uncontrolled orbital spin.

His team was now staring at him, expectantly waiting.

"GPS is still functioning, though there's little left for it to connect to—most receiving devices were rendered useless in the first few hours. The European Union, Russia, and China all have navigation satellites in mid orbit. There are communication satellites, a couple observation satellites, a few space telescopes, and some research and scientific satellites."

"That all sounds pretty useless," Paul said.

"Maybe. Maybe not. Some can be re-purposed to be more useful." He pushed on. "High Earth Orbit has communications and weather satellites—"

"Super helpful when you're in a bunker. Someone can tell us if it's going to rain outside." Roslynn's tone expressed her frustration—their frustration.

"Most HEO satellites were for interplanetary and deep space missions plus some scientific research." He lowered his voice. "The thing is, the US government commissioned some of that research."

He put the last word in air quotes.

"Could be anything," Ken said.

"Could be missile defensive systems." Paul shrugged. "Don't look at me like that. I know stuff. Plus, I saw it in a movie once, which sent me down a research rabbit hole—back in the day when we could do outside research."

"The Missile Defense Agency has maintained a presence in the Higher Earth Orbit," Gus continued. "From what I've been able to glean, nothing has come into the US airspace and nothing has gone out—yet. So far, what we're dealing with... what probably caused the event in Chicago... is either an accident or domestic terrorism."

The thought of which stole everyone's appetite. They dumped their remaining food—Gus once again thinking of the people on the outside—and went back to work. Colonel Webb had not let up one bit. Each time they turned in an analytical report, they were immediately given another assignment. Always, they briefed Webb along with the other members of the team. They worked individually on areas that touched upon their expertise, but the world had shrunk on June 6th. Completely compartmentalizing was no longer possible. What one member learned influenced another member's work.

Twelve- to fifteen-hour days were the norm, with one day blurring into another and the first week giving way to the second and the third. Before it seemed possible, they'd been in the bunker for a month. Gus tried to imagine July on the outside—no air conditioning, no refrigerated food, medicine running out, rogue groups taking control.

Those frightening thoughts were shared by the entire KESLRFTF task force. It spurred them to grab three or four hours of sleep then drag themselves out of bed and spend additional hours working on the secret project, the one that Webb hadn't asked for, and the one thing that kept Gus from falling into complete despair.

Because the news wasn't all bad.

In fact, a little of it was actually optimistic.

By overlaying geothermal data with a map of the continental United States, they were able to determine where people were moving to and where they were coming from. The urban areas emptied out pretty quickly although there were pockets of people in some suburbs—like northeast El Paso.

Ken developed a program that would assess what areas had existing supplies or a high probability of creating their own supplies—such as tillable land, good rainfall, and a sufficient population to work the land. The result was areas that held at least a chance of producing food crops before winter set in. Paul used his expertise in logistics to analyze what locations could supply the basic necessities—clean water, fuel to burn in winter, access to medical supplies. Roslynn considered urban areas that might be re-purposed to support survivors—such as the Golden Gate National Recreation Area in San Francisco and the Balcones Canyonlands Preserve in Austin.

Lastly, Gus looked at the composition of populations within an area. He created a filter that picked those most likely to work together in a cohesive, productive manner. Not just places with low violence rates, but also places that had a population with a less contentious tone. This was difficult as it required the program to scan millions of pages of newsprint, blogs, and past social media feeds. It wasn't a perfect system. But he was reasonably confident the result would be something they could use.

It didn't come together overnight.

At first, they worried it would take weeks, and then they accepted it would take months. The stress felt like an incredible weight pressing down until it might crush them. The Kessler Effect Short and Long-Range Forecast Task Force became a tight unit. All four members of the group began jogging the corridors, even gained access to a weight room where they could attempt to burn off some of their anxious energy.

And they joked about having t-shirts made with their task force name.

"It would never fit across our chests." Paul was breathing heavily, obviously not used to any type of exercise.

Ken's color actually looked better than it had the day they'd walked into Site R. "That name wouldn't fit even if this underground bunker somehow turns us into supermen."

"And women," Roslynn added.

Behind every conversation, every analysis, every line of code, ran concerns about their new self-assigned, covert project. The key was to write the programs in such a way that they overlaid one another, like putting a weather map over a car's GPS system. It sounded easy, but was incredibly difficult to do—and they weren't programmers. But they were determined. As the situation outside the bunker deteriorated and their own restlessness of being trapped underground increased, what they were attempting took on mythic proportions. During one particularly late-night session when they were loopy from lack of sleep and a little drunk on a bottle of rum Roslynn had traded her transistor radio for, they nicknamed it the NWM.

The New World Map.

It worked.

It was a thing of beauty.

Twenty-four prime locations for beginning again spread across the continental US north to south. East to west.

"I'd go," Roslynn said. "Seriously—send me. I believe this is more important than what Webb has had us doing. Damage control? There is no controlling what has happened ... what *is* happening outside these walls. But this?"

She tapped the desk that all four of their computers were crammed on. "This is a chance. It's a second chance."

They did not show their program to Webb the next day because their own particular world began falling apart.

Paul woke them in the middle of the night, moaning in his

bed, curled into a tight ball. Gus woke to find Roslynn attempting to find out what was wrong.

"Is it your stomach?"

Another groan from his bunk was followed by the sound of Paul retching. Roslynn stepped aside until he was done.

"What should we do?" Ken asked, as Gus grabbed a couple towels and attempted to wipe up the mess on the floor.

"Go get help."

"Where..."

"Find Webb. Or Kendricks. Even Lawrence." When Matt still didn't move, Gus took the young man by the shoulders. "Go to the mess hall and call out for a medic. There's bound to be one in there."

Fifteen minutes later they were rolling Paul out on a gurney.

Eighty minutes after that, Major Lawrence found them in the mess hall. "Emergency appendectomy. He's fine. If it had ruptured... Let's just say it's a good thing you called for a medic when you did."

It didn't end there though.

The next day, Ken came down with a nasty bout of influenza and had to spend a week in whatever passed for their hospital. For a while, it was only Gus and Roslynn in the room. He thought he'd enjoy the extra space, but he didn't. It felt empty.

Roslynn summed it up nicely. "I'd rather it be crowded with all four of us here."

Instead of focusing on that, they worked harder.

Refined the programs.

Perfected the overlay.

On the national scene, an ominous hush had spread across the land. The monitoring satellites in mid and upper orbit fell silent, and no one could figure out why. They were effectively in the dark, and winter had just begun.

THE PRESIDENT HAD RECORDED and attempted to broadcast monthly updates since that fateful day on June 6th. At first, there was radio chatter indicating that at least some of the American populace had heard it. Each month there was less. Perhaps they'd run out of batteries or their generators had gone dry. Perhaps no one was left to receive the broadcast. Or maybe they were too busy struggling to survive.

By January, the president was demanding answers.

Each of the underground facilities sent out scout groups with instructions to return in forty-eight hours. Most did, but what they had to report wasn't good—empty towns, deserted houses, a stunningly blue pollution-free sky, and undisturbed snow as far as they could see. Two of the groups didn't return at all. Had they gone AWOL? Simply walked away? Had they been attacked? What was the situation outside the bunkers?

They were meeting with Webb on a Thursday afternoon in February. Their group was finally back together. Paul looked no worse for his emergency surgery. Ken had lost even more weight from his bout with influenza. Roslynn sported dark circles under her eyes. Gus had no idea how he looked as he hadn't gazed into a mirror in weeks, maybe longer.

But they were together again, and perhaps that was what gave them the courage to explain what they had done.

"I'll need those reports in forty-eight hours," Webb barked. If anything, his mood had deteriorated with the extended stay below Raven Rock. He had just asked for an extended analysis on what a clearing of all debt would do to a post Kessler Effect economy.

"Maybe we're going about this all wrong," Roslynn said, not squirming or backing down when Webb pierced her with one of his cold, do-you-realize-who-you're-talking-to stares.

They'd learned that Webb's bark was indeed much worse than his bite. He'd even partook in the dwindling bottle of rum when he caught them in the mess hall late one night. Not that they ever mentioned the few minutes they'd seen the man behind the uniform. He'd looked older, exhausted, but not quite defeated.

When his glare didn't produce the desired effect, he sighed and said, "Tell me more."

"Maybe we should be focused on predicting where surviving populations would exist." Paul leaned forward in his chair. "It can be analyzed, same as everything else you've had us do."

"Forward-looking instead of past or even present." Ken's gaze had taken on a particular intensity since his illness, as if he realized his days—all of their days—were numbered.

Webb didn't answer at first, but they had clearly caught him by surprise. He stared at a point on the far wall, and finally asked, "How long would this take?"

"It's done." Gus said it quietly, but in the silence of the colonel's office, it felt as if he'd used a megaphone. "We've already done it."

They showed the integrated program to him that night.

The next morning, he had them explain it again, from the beginning, to General Kendricks.

Kendricks kicked it up the chain of command until eventually they had a green light from the president himself.

"Green light to do what?" Gus asked. They were once again back in Webb's office, though not on their normal Thursday afternoon. That, in and of itself, said something was up.

"Send teams out to the locations you pinpointed." Webb sat back in his chair, studying them.

Gus wondered why it felt like everything was about to change.

Was everything about to change?

And if so, for better or worse?

"As I told you at the beginning, there are other teams—not unlike yourselves—at other locations. Much of the work you've done has been done, simultaneously, by them. Not only did that provide us with redundancy should one of the bunkers be breached, but it also provided confirmation. Within a point or two, your reports were identical with each other." Webb reached for a bottle of water, drank half of it, then nodded at Gus's computer that sat centered on his desk. "No one else came up with that."

Gus looked to Roslyn, then Paul and Ken. Finally, he said, "We don't know what that means."

"It means that you did a fine job, and we're going to allow you to have your pick of locations."

Roslynn half rose out of her chair. "Our pick?"

"Small units will be deployed near these sites. They'll perform reconnaissance and then make contact. And you four are going. You four can choose which site you want to travel to."

"Why?" Ken asked.

Webb studied them for a moment before answering. "It isn't merely your ability with a computer that makes you perfect for this assignment, though that's a definite plus. Just as important, you're different. You think differently. You analyze, sure. But you also problem-solve in a more real-world frame than many in the military. So, which will it be? Which site do you choose?"

"Boulder, Colorado," Roslynn said, then glanced at the others. "Unless one of you wants it."

Ken was staring at the display on the computer screen. Twenty-four pinpoints. Twenty-four possibilities. Twenty-four places where they might be able to start over and this time maybe they'd get it right. "Cody, Wyoming," he said, his voice soft but sure.

"I've always wanted to see apple orchards." Paul tapped his fingers against his chair. "I'll take Hood River, Oregon."

Gus heard them. He became aware they were all watching him, but he had the strange sensation that this was something that had happened before. Maybe he'd dreamed it. Maybe it was his destiny. Regardless, he knew his answer. He met Webb's gaze and said, "Alpine, Texas."

He'd never been to Texas.

Hadn't visited much of the southwest at all.

But he'd known, months ago, that the little town in the Chihuahuan Desert—just over a hundred miles from the Chisos Mountains, Big Bend National Park, the Mexican border—had captured his imagination. He'd gradually become aware, that if he had a chance to do it all again, he would pick that little southwest corner of Texas.

They left three weeks later.

CHAPTER 4

Gus drew in his first lungful of fresh air on March 7th, just over nine months after the satellites fell. Colonel Webb had escorted them out of the bunker. The day was cold but cloudless. The rugged terrain of the Blue Ridge Mountains stretched into the distance. Gus could make out oak, maple, even hickory trees. He could hear the gurgling of a nearby stream. He closed his eyes, breathed deeply, and vowed never to take for granted the freedom of being out in the open.

Webb waited until they'd turned their attention back to him. "I want to thank each of you. The work you've done here... obviously you went above and beyond. I'm proud of you. Proud of each one of you." He shook their hands, tears shining in the old colonel's eyes, and then he said something about the cold air affecting his allergies and strode off.

"I knew he'd soften up," Paul murmured. "Just didn't think it would take until our last morning here."

Gus didn't know what to say. He still couldn't quite

comprehend that he was outside. That he was about to leave this place. It all felt surreal, like a dream within a dream.

"Having second thoughts?" Roslynn asked.

"Not even one."

"Same." She attempted a smile, then threw her arms around him.

Gus smelled her hair, breathed in the scent of her, realized that she was his first true friend in quite a while.

"Thank you," she said.

"For?"

"Playing gin rummy with me? Not snoring? Coming up with this idea to begin with?" She stepped back, swiped at her eyes, and hitched up her backpack. "Basically everything."

"We were a good team," Paul said, smiling at them as he pulled on the winter gloves he'd been issued.

"We *are* a good team," Ken corrected. "And we're actually doing this. We're testing our hypothesis as well as the code we wrote. We're in the real world now."

They turned and looked out at what had been Raven Rock Township. Although they understood the numbers and percentages, though they'd seen the footage and even heard some of the early revolts, they still weren't quite prepared for the difference in the view of the surrounding area this bright morning, especially compared to what they'd seen nine months earlier.

No vehicles.

No people.

The concertina wire surrounding Site R had been ripped away.

Someone had spray-painted the word *Fallen* on the pavement.

Fallen?

What did it mean? Society had fallen? Humanity had

fallen? Gus thought maybe it didn't mean anything. Maybe it was done by a teen with a can of spray paint needing to leave his mark.

Several inches of snow lay unblemished by human footprints.

Where had everyone gone?

Were they being watched?

Would they be attacked as they tried to leave?

Someone hollered, "Attention!" and as one, they turned toward General Kendricks. He didn't stand in the bed of a truck. He didn't need a bullhorn. He surveyed the eighty people who would be leaving the shelter of Raven Rock.

Eighty people sent out in four different directions.

Four groups of twenty, which included an analyst, a commanding officer, a medic, a mechanic, and sixteen soldiers.

They'd travel light in the hopes of passing unnoticed and making good time.

"I cannot overstate the importance of your journey. If these United States of America are to exist as a single body again, it will be necessary to set up regional centers. As you're aware, other COG facilities are also sending out teams. There will be twenty-four in all. From Raven Rock, there will be four." General Kendricks hesitated, let his gaze drift over them as a pained look temporarily crossed his face.

His voice grew softer, and Gus found himself leaning forward to be certain to catch each word. "Your journey will not be easy. You are in no way prepared—emotionally or physically—for what you will encounter. How does one prepare him or herself for the apocalypse?"

He straightened his posture, and his voice grew stronger, more commanding. "And yet, I believe you will succeed. While you are traveling to your assignment, men and women in COG centers across this country will continue to work on reestablishing communication, basic services, and a manufacturing/supply chain. We will not rest until we are able to once again meet the needs of the American people. We will not rest until that flag—"

Now they turned and gazed in the direction that Kendricks was pointing, toward the top of the RRMC facility.

Gus hadn't seen the stars and stripes.

He'd been busy looking the other direction, looking for any sign of life. Now, he felt a surge of patriotism unlike any he'd ever felt before. How many times had he taken that flag for granted? Even as he'd sung the national anthem at a baseball game, or driven past flags displayed down the main thoroughfares during Memorial Day. The White House. The capitol building. Washington's Monument. He'd taken all of those sightings of this symbol of freedom for granted. His mind had barely registered their presence.

He would never take it for granted again.

"No one in this government will rest until that flag is once more flown across America. May you travel without hindrance, arrive in good time, and facilitate a successful coalition with the people in your area. Godspeed." General Kendricks snapped off a salute, and they were dismissed.

Ken took off his glasses and wiped at his eyes.

Paul cleared his throat and cinched up his pack.

Roslynn said, "I'd tell you guys to write, but in all likelihood that wouldn't be possible and we'll probably never see each other again, so—"

"Hey." Gus stopped her. "We did this together. We created this plan, and it's going to work. When it does, we'll celebrate —together. I don't know where and I don't know when, but we will be together again."

"I'll bring the rum," Paul said. "Or maybe cold beer."

"And I'll bring the pizza." Ken plastered on a grin. "Extra cheese."

They came together in one giant, messy hug, and then—before anyone had a chance to lose the tenuous grip on his or her emotions completely—they broke apart and walked off to join their individual groups.

They'd done the numbers one last time the night before.

Roslynn would have the shortest journey at sixteen hundred miles to Boulder. She would travel through Ohio, Indiana, Missouri, and Kansas before arriving in Colorado.

Gus's route was slightly longer at just over eighteen hundred miles, six hundred and fifty of which would be crossing Texas from the northeast to the southwest.

Ken's path would take him nineteen hundred miles, skirting the Great Lakes, then passing through Wisconsin, Southern Illinois, and South Dakota. It might have been more prudent to wait until the snows in the northern states melted, but everyone in his team had agreed it was better to go now—less traffic, less chance of an altercation if everyone was still holed up trying to stay warm.

Paul had the longest trip at nearly twenty-seven hundred miles. He would practically be traveling coast to coast, though he would be starting two hundred miles west of the Atlantic Ocean and ending just one hundred and forty-two miles shy of the Pacific.

Each team would travel in groups of five vehicles—four persons per vehicle. They could have fit into fewer, but the US Army was following through on its insistence for redundancy. If one truck broke down, they'd consolidate. If two broke down, they could still make it. Left unsaid was what they'd do if they ended up with only one or even zero vehicles.

Of course, the group had run analytical tables on their odds of success. If they could complete the trip in the vehicles, their odds of reaching their destination clicked in at seventy-two percent. Not as high as they'd like, but better than fifty-fifty.

If, for whatever reason, they ended up having to walk then the odds dropped dramatically. One model put their odds of success at eight percent, and that was the best scenario.

Gus had never been much of a praying man, not since he'd spent summers with his grandparents and attended old-fashioned revival meetings. But as he climbed into his group's G-wagen, the military variant of a Mercedes-Benz G-Class, he said a silent prayer.

At this point, he didn't see how it could hurt.

THE G-WAGEN HAD excellent off-road capability, better fuel consumption than the Humvee, and was easier to maneuver through urban areas than the Unimog. It was also extremely expensive, and it wasn't like anyone would be making additional vehicles anytime soon. Still, when the KESLRFTF Task Force had asked for it, the Army had instantly complied.

In fact, they'd agreed to every request, which should have been the first clue that what they were doing was even more dangerous than Gus and his group anticipated it to be. In the back of his mind, he knew that the government wasn't telling them everything. They never told a single person every detail, not even the president. But he trusted their superiors to tell members of the KESLRFTF what they needed to know in order to make an accurate assessment.

Maybe that was true.

Maybe not.

Gus's team headed southwest out of Liberty Township. They passed a few abandoned cars, some burned-out buildings, more graffiti claiming *The End is Now* and *Blame AI* and even *They Walk Among Us*. He wasn't sure what that last one meant unless it was referring to aliens. The next forty-five minutes were basically a smooth ride. Gus traveled in a vehicle with the team lead, Sergeant Major Aimee Taylor. She was Black, maybe thirty-five years old, and no-nonsense. Gus was sure she could kick his ass, despite the fact that he'd actually put on a little more muscle while inside Raven Rock. Taylor looked hardcore army.

Gavin Montgomery was Caucasian, twenty-two years old, and was considered to be an expert medic, having already served overseas on active duty. At twenty-two years old? Gus wondered about the state of their world even before the satellites had fallen. To think that an enlisted person could gain adequate experience by such a young age... that seemed like an ominous thing to him. Gavin was from Alabama, and he seemed friendly enough.

Ryan Sorrell had yet to speak. He was maybe close to thirty and of indeterminate ethnic heritage, though if pressed Gus would guess Hispanic or maybe European. Sorrell was the sharp-shooter of their team. The guy's gaze seemed to take in everything. His focus was laser-like, and he'd simply nodded when Gus said hello.

They'd been on the road less than thirty minutes when they attempted to merge onto I-70, which would take them through Hagerstown, then allow them to exit to I-81S. A northern route would have taken them through Charleston and Lexington. The southern route was definitely the better choice. Both routes merged together in Nashville—what the Task Force had labeled a choke point.

Like many urban centers, Nashville had in recent years experienced a dramatic increase in cost of living. An analytical survey indicated contention between long-term residents, tourism, and people who had recently moved to the area. June

6th would have trapped all three groups together in a stressful, frightening situation. There were other concerns about Music City USA. Education was subpar in some parts of the city, though it was fine in others. Affordable healthcare was a problem and crime rates had increased in recent years.

Every group that was sent out to the twenty-four sites on the New World Map had to pass through such an area. For Gus's group, Nashville was the first of several choke points. Nashville would be a problem.

But it wouldn't be a problem unless they made it around Hagerstown.

Montgomery was driving, but he'd slammed the vehicle to a stop at their first sight of I-70. Behind them, the other four vehicles with their team also came to an abrupt halt. The highway in front of them was literally filled with cars—all of them abandoned.

"Talk about an apocalyptic scene." Montgomery sounded a bit overwhelmed. They'd all talked about what had happened on the outside, and most had seen video footage, but looking at it in real life... that was a different thing entirely.

"Looks like everyone was trying to get out of Dodge," Taylor said. "Can we go south?"

"Negative." Sorrell's voice was clipped, as if he were saving every extra ounce of energy should he need to pounce.

Pivoting to look south, Gus saw that direction was also blocked.

Taylor turned around in her seat to stare at Gus. "Suggestions?"

He knew this route. He had memorized this route. "There's a fair network of secondary roads to the east. We'll skirt Shenandoah National Park. At Interstate 64 we'll have to make a decision. West to Staunton or east to Charlottesville." He didn't like either of those choices. They'd add miles to their trip, meaning they'd waste more fuel. Even more concerning, there was less video surveillance of what they'd find when they reached those areas.

Then again, their video surveillance of Hagerstown certainly hadn't indicated the massive pile-up they were staring at. When confronted with two bad decisions, listen to your gut and move on. "Go back a few miles, then maneuver southeast on the secondary roads."

"Do it," Taylor said.

Montgomery radioed the plan to the G-wagens behind them. They managed to turn the caravan around and rerouted to the southeast. Several times they could only make progress by pushing other vehicles out of the way. More than once, Taylor, Montgomery, and Gus had exited their vehicle, where they were joined by persons from the other four vehicles. Together they pushed cars out of the way. It was the first time that Gus encountered bodies. They looked to have been shot. For their money? Supplies? Certainly not for the vehicle as it had been left there.

As they moved the cars, Sorrell had stood guard over them, his gaze constantly swiveling left to right—then right to left, his weapon at the ready. Their progress was incredibly slow, but they did continue moving in the right direction.

Until they came across their first group of survivors.

They'd made it to a town called Front Royal, just south of Highway 66. Gus calculated they'd traveled 84 miles, and it had taken over four hours. At this rate, it would take ten days to arrive in Alpine. They could do it faster if they traveled at night, but doing so would exponentially increase their risk level. The plan was to travel each day to the next fuel cache, spend the night, then leave before daylight.

Gus understood that plans were simply that—an attempt to predict what might happen. Looking at the group of people positioned across the road at Front Royal, he realized that the plan had once again changed. He'd known they'd run into survivors. He hadn't pictured how vulnerable and desperate they'd be.

"Stop the vehicle," he said, leaning forward so that Montgomery could clearly hear him.

"Not advisable," Sorrell muttered.

Taylor turned to pierce him with a gaze. "Our mission is to take you to Alpine and set up one of the regional government headquarters."

"Our mission is to help the people who survived. These people are survivors, and they quite obviously need our help."

Gus wasn't looking at Taylor when he said it. Maybe he was speaking to everyone in the vehicle. Maybe he was speaking to himself.

He was looking out the window at a young mother, holding an infant in her arms. An infant. How had they survived winter? All of the people surrounding their tight group of five vehicles looked gaunt, exhausted. They plainly were not a threat. It was a strange thing being a contractor with the military. You were a part of the greater body and yet separate from it. Gus had no rank. He wasn't enlisted or commissioned, but he was in charge of this team. Both Webb and Kendricks had made that abundantly clear to all involved. The KESLRFTF had conceived, created, and presented the New World Map. All decisions related to the missions were theirs to make unless they deferred to another member of the group.

Gus was not deferring.

This was his call to make.

"Stop the vehicle," he repeated.

Three of them exited slowly—Taylor, Sorrell, and Gus. Montgomery stayed behind the wheel and kept the G-wagen idling. When Sorrell stepped out, weapon at the ready, the crowd took a step back. But they didn't run. They needed help that badly, so badly that a loaded weapon pointed in their direction wasn't enough to dissuade them.

An older man moved forward. His white beard had been trimmed, his hair cut if raggedly so, and he looked surprisingly fit. "My name is Otis Jones, and we need your help."

Gus introduced himself, then the rest of the team. They followed Otis to the center of the town, which looked like the center of a thousand other towns across the country—a regal courthouse dominated the square, stores and restaurants rimmed the downtown area. The people, what remained of the residents of Front Royal, had banded together, managed to drive off would-be assailants, and helped those who needed help—even when their own supplies dwindled.

"Now we're out," Otis admitted. "We've begun to plant things, but that food won't be ready in time to help us."

"Have you scavenged the area?" Taylor asked.

"As far as we dare. Plus, we've taken advantage of local game." Otis shook his head. Less than fifty Front Royal residents were gathered for the impromptu meeting.

"Is this all that's left?" Gus asked.

"Yeah. We had fifteen thousand people before June 6th."

"What happened to them?" Montgomery might have seen similar things when he'd served overseas, but plainly it was a shock for him to see such a situation in his own country.

"Some left. Thought it would be better elsewhere. Some fled into the Shenandoah National Park to the south. The forty-eight souls you see here are all that's left."

Gus fought the urge to say they'd stay, they'd help, they'd share from their provisions. He wanted to do all those things, but he also understood that Taylor had been correct—their primary goal was Alpine.

"I need to speak with my team," Gus said. "Privately."

Otis nodded and suggested they use the judge's chambers.

Like most of the rooms they'd passed in the courthouse, it had been turned into sleeping quarters. Mattresses, no doubt pulled from nearby homes, lined the walls. Blankets were pulled up or neatly straightened. A row of baby dolls lay across the pillow of one bed.

Gus turned and faced his team. "I want to hear your opinion. Do we stay and help these people?"

Taylor was for moving on.

Sorrell saw the stop as a needless additional risk.

Montgomery, who was their driver but also their medic, was on Gus's side. "I can help them. Let me at least look at the ones who are sick, see what can be done."

"Why?" Taylor's glare was fierce. "Why would we do that?"

"Because they're Americans." Gus held up a hand to stop her protest. "I understand the pros and cons, but if we can't stop and help these people then what are we even doing out here? We might as well have stayed hunkered down safely inside Raven Rock."

Sorrell's frown grew more pronounced, so what he said next completely surprised Gus. "There's a supply cache thirty miles from here. I could go, take a few guys from the other vehicles with me, get the fuel we need, and bring back some food for Front Royal. We can't give them a lot—there's not that much space in the G-wagens and we need provisions, too—but it might be enough to get them through until their crops are ready."

"Two vehicles only," Taylor said. "If you're not back in twelve hours, we leave without you."

Gus was nodding before she even finished talking. "That will work. Thanks. I appreciate the risk you're taking, and I also appreciate your accepting my leadership."

"It's not a question of accepting your leadership." Taylor

squeezed the bridge of her nose. Finally, she looked at Gus. "This is the US Army. You are leading this group, whether you want to or not—whether you're qualified or not. Our orders were clear. We are following you, because that is what we were ordered to do. That's the way the Army functions. But I want you to remember something. These people in Front Royal aren't the only lives you're responsible for."

They set off in different directions then.

Gus to inform Otis of their plan.

Montgomery to set up a triage center.

Sorrel approached the other four vehicles to ask for volunteers to go to the supply cache and back.

Gus realized that they weren't a cohesive group. Not yet. Not like the KESLRFTF had become. But he thought they might be... eventually.

They stayed in Front Royal for three days. They made similar stops throughout Virginia and into Tennessee. Nashville wasn't the problem Gus thought it would be. Everything was wrecked, vandalized, burned. What remained standing was covered with graffiti.

Deserted.

Forgotten.

Music Row and Hillsboro Pike and Elliston Place had all been left for whatever or whoever came next. Several times they passed plane wreckage, and twice he looked out the G-wagen's windows to see what looked like satellite debris. Western Tennessee was filled with small towns of people needing help. Each time they repeated what they'd done in Front Royal. They helped as they could, and then they moved on. Most stops went well, but two went tragically wrong.

Twice, the Alpine Group, as they'd begun to refer to themselves, were attacked by rebel forces. Sorrell's aim was true. There was no pause for negotiation. When someone threatened their convoy, Sorrell neutralized the threat. One of those times, near Memphis, Tennessee, turned into a short-lived battle. Short-lived because Sorrell and the other armed soldiers took out the opposing forces quickly.

Hot Springs was even worse. They'd attempted to navigate around the town, but had been ambushed by a well-armed group of insurgents. The Alpine Group prevailed after nearly an hour of frenzied shooting, but three of their own were killed and they lost one of the vehicles owing to the tires being shot out.

The danger seemed to be growing.

Taylor insisted that Gus carry a firearm. She also issued her first ultimatum. "I need to know that you know how to use it, Martinez. We are tasked with protecting you, but I have to know that you can protect yourself."

"Or what?" It was a stupid thing to say. He was tired, stressed, and felt unreasonably stubborn.

Taylor moved right up into his personal space. She might have been an inch shorter, but she was immeasurably tougher. "Do not force me to make a decision we'll both regret."

Gus felt stupid wasting ammunition on target practice, but after three rounds through Taylor's makeshift target, she held up her hand for him to stop.

"You're good," she said. "Better than I expected."

They'd left Raven Rock on March 24th, and they didn't reach the Texas border until the first of May. Were the other groups that had left Raven Rock encountering this much resistance? He attempted to check in with Colonel Webb on a regular basis but many times the call from his satellite phone didn't go through. Webb didn't share how the other groups were doing, and Gus didn't ask. He was afraid to ask. He'd rather wait until Webb burst with the good news that the other twenty-three groups were in place. Or maybe he'd simply bark, "What's your problem, Martinez? Everyone else has done this, and so can you. I order you to be successful."

Yes. He would be happy to hear either of those things.

Two-thirds of their journey was behind them, and Dallas was directly ahead. The Dallas-Fort Worth metropolitan area had been home to more than seven million people on June 6th.

It was worse than he'd imagined. Even the outer ring of suburbs resembled a desolate cityscape—crumbling buildings, abandoned vehicles, an air of emptiness and decay. Stores were looted and churches had been burned to the ground. Entire neighborhoods of homes were now merely piles of rubble.

Graffiti was everywhere, like a dying town's last words.

The scene grew more desperate as they approached. They came across their first hanging bodies, wearing cardboard placards that read

Go back or you're next

Gus called for a team meeting.

The vote was unanimous.

Detour south.

It would add weeks on their journey, but at least they had a chance of arriving intact.

He attempted to radio their new route into Raven Rock, with no luck. The satellite phones were a constant frustration. They represented the hope they weren't in this alone, but increasingly they didn't work. Intellectually, Gus understood why. He could picture the debris field, and he understood that even now—nearly a year after the event—objects and satellites continued to orbit in an uncontrolled manner. It was honestly surprising the SAT phones worked at all. Though some of the government satellites remained functional in upper orbit, communication was spotty and unreliable. The few messages they'd received from General Kendricks indicated that skirmishes between rebel forces were ongoing. Some of those forces appeared to be growing in size as spring turned to summer.

May in Texas felt like summer. The Lone Star State enjoyed a long growing season that often stretched from March to November. It was one of the things in the plus column for Alpine. But with those long, warm months came oppressive heat often accompanied by drought. A deadly combination that meant rebel forces, even survivor groups that had previously been unaggressive, were becoming increasingly violent.

They detoured through Longview, Tyler, Waco.

By the time they angled toward the southwest corner of the state, encounters with survivor groups grew more and more rare, then stopped altogether. When they reached the Chihuahuan Desert, Sergeant Major Aimee Taylor twisted around in her seat and gave Gus a pointed look.

"Are you sure there's anyone left in this corner of the world?"

"Yeah. I'm sure." Gus trusted the program that he and Roslynn and Paul and Ken had created. "Someone's there."

The date was May 26th when they turned south toward Alpine.

CHAPTER 5

J une 6
Alpine, Texas
One year after the Satellites Fell

THE PEOPLE of Alpine voted to activate the beacon.

Police Chief Tanda Lopez had mixed feelings about that.

She paused in front of the mirror in the restroom at the Alpine Police Station. She was acutely aware that she still represented the Alpine Police Department. She represented law and order. Her uniform was reasonably clean, as clean as something could be that you hand-washed once a week. Her duty belt rested comfortably on her slim hips. She mentally ticked off her equipment.

Flashlight—a small, light version that shone over 200 lumens. They were down to their last box of batteries.

Handcuffs—something she hadn't used in quite some time, but best to be prepared.

needed to convey a sense of certainty. As a citizen, she harbored a nauseating sense of dread in her gut.

"I'm still not convinced this is the best way to go."

"The vote was nearly unanimous," Logan reminded her. "Only Joshua Andrews and Peggy Looper voted against it."

"Peggy, I understand. She's headed up the Legacy Project from the beginning of this thing. She has a broader conception of the status of things."

"More reasons to be wary."

"Exactly. She's heard firsthand the stories of people stumbling into Alpine, running from rebel forces, running from paramilitary forces. But Joshua..."

"His injury has taken a toll on the man." Logan held up his hand when she turned on him. "I'm not saying he's less. I'm saying he's different."

"True enough. Though we didn't actually know him before."

Joshua had suffered a debilitating injury while traveling from Dallas to Alpine. He was an integral part of their community now—mechanical engineer, beekeeper, philosopher.

"I asked him why he'd voted against activating the beacon." Logan touched her arm, halting their progress.

"What did he say?"

"Not much. Shook his head and assured me he'd support the majority whichever way the vote went."

"You're worried he knows something we don't."

"I have no doubt he knows things we don't, but in this case I think it's just an intuition..." He paused and looked out over the crowd. "Or maybe just a fear. Sometimes it's hard to separate one from the other."

They resumed walking in silence. Tanda had never felt more comfortable with anyone than she did with Logan. She supposed repeatedly facing death together had something to do with that. She'd only admitted to herself that she loved him two months ago, and she'd only spoken the words aloud twice. She probably needed to learn to be more open with her feelings, but Logan seemed to understand that her reticence wasn't about him.

As they approached the lawn surrounding the gazebo, Tanda hung back. "I'm worried his intuition is right and ours is wrong."

"Our intuition is largely formed from our experiences." Logan turned his back on the crowd and lowered his voice. "Both Peggy and Joshua didn't trust the government in the best of times. It's understandable they wouldn't want to bring said forces into town now."

Tanda nodded. Her thoughts, as usual, pulled in two directions. On the one hand, this beacon could be what saved them through what looked to be a long, hot, dry summer. On the other hand, she could relate to Peggy and Joshua.

When had the government really helped them?

Where had they been on June 6th?

What had they been doing in the intervening year?

The vote to activate the beacon had been quick and definitive. More contentious than the vote itself was the decision of when to push the button. Four of the survivors from the human Faraday cage in Van Horn had taken up residence in Alpine. The head of that group, Perry Reed, had been for activating it immediately. "Pull the Band-Aid off quick," he'd said with a shrug and smile.

But it was Felicia who had suggested the idea that the anniversary of the phenomena known as the Kessler Effect would be the right time for such drastic measures. Tanda liked the symmetry in that. And maybe a part of her had hoped that in the time between the vote and June 6th, the decision would be taken away from them.

That hadn't happened.

So it was that on June 6th, nearly everyone in Alpine Texas gathered around the old gazebo. Both the setting and the mood reminded Tanda of that evening after the fall of the satellites, when they had gathered for a grand town picnic, choosing to grill and share all the food in their freezers before it went bad. Had that actually been almost a year ago? It was difficult for her to accept all that happened in the last twelve months.

"I know what you're thinking," Logan said.

"Unless you've developed Felicia's powers of second sight, I strongly doubt that." Tanda let her gaze linger on his. How had she fallen for this man so completely and so suddenly? He'd been her close friend for all of her life, and then suddenly in one moment when he wavered between life and death, he'd become more.

Logan reached for her hand. "Fine, Police Chief Tanda Lopez. Maybe I don't know what you're thinking, but I have a pretty good guess."

"Yeah?"

"Sure. You're thinking the same thing we're all thinking. A year ago we couldn't have imagined ourselves living in this situation, having won in some ways and lost in so many others."

"It's the losses that haunt me the most."

"I know."

"How long do you think it will take?"

"Are you asking me if the US government is going to swoop in between now and sunset? I highly doubt that."

"Agreed."

"So maybe we just enjoy this moment of hope."

Tanda and Logan wound their way through the crowd, climbed the steps of the gazebo, and joined the Council.

Everyone seemed in high spirits, but Tanda felt as if she had the uncanny ability to see past that momentary enthusiasm to the worries and exhaustion lurking beneath. She knew and cared for each person on the lawn, as well as those gathered on the stage. They had become family.

Ron Mullins—previously their public works director, he had been mere months from retirement when the world had changed.

Dixie Peters—fire chief who lost her fiancé on the day of the event. At least, that's what they all assumed since he hadn't been seen or heard from.

Emmanuel Garcia—county health commissioner who was still attempting to perform the duties of that job, albeit in a vastly different way.

Miles Turner had been hiding out in a cabin on Old Ranch Road when Tanda had first visited him, alerting him to the town's desperate need for another doctor. His dog Zeus lay faithfully next to him, surveying the crowd with a dopey smile.

Harper Moore held six-week-old Kai in her arms. Harper had come from El Paso and nearly died on the trip. She and Cade and Liam had literally fought their way to Alpine. Tanda felt as if she'd known them all her life.

Her brother Keme nodded as she sat beside him. No doubt he was thinking of Lucy, of his own personal loss, and wondering why it had to happen.

Gonzo Watson had initially represented the local artisan group. Now he simply represented Alpine.

Sitting on Tanda's other side was Logan. The man was like a freaking lighthouse in a storm.

Ron, Dixie, Emanuel.

Miles, Harper, and Keme.

Gonzo.

Logan and Tanda.

Together the nine constituted the Council, a duly elected body of leaders charged with guiding and protecting Alpine. All carried the terrible burden of caring for the group before them and ensuring the survival of this town. The original leadership group had included Keme's wife, Lucy, and Jackson, a local rancher. Both had died defending Alpine, as had many others.

Tanda couldn't do a thing about their shared, tragic past.

What plagued her... what had kept her awake many nights... was the fear that this step they were taking might be pointing them in the wrong direction. One that would be difficult, or perhaps impossible, to correct. And yet, maybe this would be a turning point toward a better life.

Keme moved to the front and center of the stage, and the crowd immediately quieted. Keme was forty-six years old, twelve years older than Tanda. She thought he physically represented their Apache-Hispanic background more than she did. They both had black hair that they wore in a long braid down their backs. His frame was tall and wiry, while she was only five foot, four inches and her weight had dropped to 120 pounds. Deep lines were etched across his face giving it a chiseled appearance, but it was his eyes that set Keme apart. They were calm but tragic, serious, imploring. Tanda didn't see those traits in her own reflection—she only saw exhaustion and a little confusion.

"We all understand why we're here today," Keme said. "Before we get into activating this beacon, I want to update you on the group to the north of town. Patrols are keeping an eye for any movement toward Alpine—there hasn't been any. As far as we can tell, it's probably a group moving west toward El Paso or maybe east toward the Hill Country."

"Wouldn't want to be in their shoes," someone from the back of the group called.

"Agreed. As long as they make no move toward Alpine, we won't intercept."

Tanda watched the people of Alpine. All seemed satisfied with Keme's explanation. The group to the north was one reason she wasn't sleeping well. They probably weren't a threat, but until they were gone she would be on edge.

"Now back to the beacon." Keme waited for the conversations to die down. When they did, he continued."We agreed that today was the day we would take this step into the unknown. Whatever happens after this, we—the Council—want you to know that we could not be prouder of how this town has pulled together and supported one another. We might be just a small speck in the southwest corner of Texas, but we found a way to survive."

Dylan Spencer called from the back of the crowd, "With deer meat and spring water, but we survived."

To this, the crowd laughed and some of the tension bled out of the air.

Tanda's gaze sought and found Aisha Nkosi. She'd been the physician for the group of scientists trapped in the Orion Orbital Solutions habitat. When they were rescued by Liam and Felicia, Aisha had opted to travel to Pecos in search of her parents. She'd returned disheartened and exhausted. She hadn't found them. She hadn't found anyone. Pecos, once a town of thirteen thousand, was nothing more than charred buildings and empty streets. When she had described this to the Council, each member had nodded in understanding. Many of the Council had seen similar instances of exactly the same thing.

Fort Davis—burned to the ground.

Marfa, which wasn't big in the best of times—abandoned.

Marathon—a ghost town.

Two months ago they'd sent scouts north to Fort Stockton.

They'd returned and reported the once bustling town was also virtually abandoned. Whether that had been by choice or by need, no one really knew.

Aisha turned to Perry Reed, the commander of the Orion crew, and touched his arm.

Perry had given them the device that would supposedly call for help. Now, he joined them in the gazebo. Tanda thought that he looked both older and yet better than he had when he'd first come to Alpine. Older because the weight of this decision seemed to rest on his shoulders. Even though he had left it to the Council to decide, left it to the people to vote on, no one knew what activating the tracker would do. He'd shared with Tanda that he would feel responsible if things went badly.

She'd assured him that wasn't the case. They would decide together and accept the blame together—there was plenty of blame to go around for all that had gone wrong in the last year.

Tanda pulled her attention back to the present as Perry climbed the steps and stopped center stage. Keme turned and accepted the box from Gonzo.

Perry squared his shoulders and addressed the crowd. "As the person who brought this Pandora's box into your town, the Council thought it might be appropriate for me to say a few words. But like you, I mostly have questions. Could things go badly? Yup. Could they also go well? Again—yes. Or—"

"More of nothing," Liam Contreras called out. As someone who had been working for the military only six months ago, he'd told Tanda this was the most likely outcome.

"I didn't vote for or against this step," Perry continued. "Honestly, I didn't feel it was my place. But Liam is correct. It's possible that absolutely nothing will happen."

Perry paused and searched the crowd as if he needed to memorize these people and this moment. "The Council has talked about that in-depth. There seems to be no danger in nothing happening, other than robbing us of the hope that someone else, someone in charge, might still be out there. Effectively we wouldn't be any worse off than we are now."

Tanda noticed several nodding in agreement, which perhaps gave Perry the encouragement he needed to continue.

"As much as we'd all like to see an immediate return to air conditioning, refrigeration, and medical supplies, I can't quite envision that. Even if the US government rolled through town twenty minutes from now, they wouldn't be able to bring those things."

The grid was down.

Resurrecting it would take massive resources and time.

The lack of modern conveniences had taken a toll and been more than difficult. Many with compromised health conditions hadn't survived the change. But as to those who had—they were tougher, stronger, perhaps a little wiser.

"There's an even-odds possibility that instead of calling the US government, this device will alert my former boss. I suppose I know Isaac Thornfield as well as any man can. He's rich with an over-inflated ego and unlimited resources. He's also smart, brilliant even. If anyone managed to survive the collapse of civilization, he probably did."

"He certainly left the folks in your group to fend for themselves," Conor Johnson said. Conor was Tanda's youngest officer. He'd matured in the last year. He no longer resembled the kid she had hired.

"Yup," Perry agreed. "He did. Whether that was because he couldn't monitor our situation or because it didn't seem expedient to his bottom line, I couldn't say. If it weren't for Liam and Felicia we would have died in that biodome."

The crowd was now completely silent, hanging on Perry's every word.

"The government possibility is far more serious than the first two, in my opinion. Nothing happening? We can handle that. My ex-boss, we can handle. But there's a chance that activating this beacon could bring in what remains of the US government."

Liam Contreras had repeatedly driven home this point, and Tanda understood why. He had seen the tent cities north of Guadalupe Mountain National Park that held citizens against their will. He understood firsthand what a desperate government could and would do to survive. If that had even been the government. How could they know? Unless you hiked to the encampment and knocked on a tent flap, which they—wisely —had not done.

"I'm not a doctor or a Council member. I've only been here a few months. But I understand that we desperately need medical supplies, food, even a way to defend ourselves."

Ammunition was so scarce that they no longer used it for hunting game. Instead, they had resorted to bow hunting and trapping. Should they be attacked again, they would have very little to defend themselves with—another thing that kept Tanda up at night.

"Which is a terribly long-winded way to say, I think that you all have decided well. I think you've made the difficult decision that had to be made. And regardless what happens, I will stand with you in the coming days."

He turned toward Keme, who held the box that contained the beacon. Thornfield had left it with the habitat people to use when they exited the biodome. But when that happened, when they were rescued, they no longer trusted their ability to make that choice clearly. So they'd given the device to Liam and Felicia, who had given it to Tanda, who had given it to the Council.

The crowd again grew completely quiet. Every man,

woman, and probably most of the children understood what was at stake. Keme opened the box. Perry put his hand on the red button and pushed it. In that moment, it felt to Tanda as if they were all collectively holding their breath.

And then Dylan called out, "It's not as if we expected them to drop out of the sky."

With the deed done, those assembled seemed to relax.

"Time to eat," someone called.

"I'm starving."

"You're always starving."

Pastor Tobias raised a hand and in his booming voice said, "Let's ask God to bless this meal."

Some in the crowd were part of his flock from before the collapse. Some had never considered religion before but had found it since. Others were still on the fence, which Tanda supposed described her.

But as one, they bowed their heads.

The good preacher had learned to keep it short. "Pray with me."

Memories washed over Tanda. She remembered the pastor standing beside the long row of graves after the Marfa Battle. She remembered him going with her to try and help the alcoholics and drug-dependent that they had settled into the old Maverick Inn. She remembered him standing beside Cade and Harper and baby Kai and whispering a blessing. Tanda wasn't sure that she believed everything the pastor did, but she was sure that he was a good man. She didn't think a prayer could hurt. Who could say? It might actually help.

"Guide us, Father. Protect us. Bless this food and these people."

A hearty *amen* echoed through the crowd.

The rain had been sporadic through the spring and into the beginning of summer, but still, they had plenty of vegetables, a small amount of meat, even some wine that old Mrs. Simpson had managed to ferment in her bathtub.

The crowd broke up into smaller groups. They partook of the potluck, meager as it was. They swapped stories of missed rabbits and antelope brought down with a bow. Someone began strumming a guitar, and a few of the older couples, then some of the teens, began to dance. Logan raised an eyebrow and held out his hand.

Tanda wasn't one to dance. She had spent the last year completely focused on her job, on protecting these people, on maintaining law and order. Those impulses had only grown stronger in the last year. She was—literally—always on duty.

But when Logan held out his hand, those thoughts fled. Instead, she remembered strapping him into his saddle. Leading his horse through that terrible storm. The trail of blood. Sitting by his side and weeping, convinced she was about to lose him.

Those memories were still sharp and painful and tender.

So she put her hand in his and followed him to an area that had once sported grass but was now merely dirt. It would have to stand in place of a dance floor. Tanda let herself relax in his arms, and for a few moments, she was not the cop, the chief of police, the defender of law and order. For a few moments, she was a woman, enjoying the Texas night with the man she loved.

Dixie Peters hadn't wanted to be a member of the Council, but she'd been unable to refuse. Tanda had insisted the town needed her to step up. She'd felt it was enough that she was tasked with keeping a town from burning with no water. Add to that the fact that her fiancé had disappeared immediately after the events of June 6th, and she didn't feel in a position to lead anyone.

And yet, she had accepted the added burden almost a year ago. She still wasn't comfortable with it.

The afternoon following the activation of the beacon, she stood with her back resting against a tree, staring at the box that had been left on a small table in the center of the gazebo.

"Maybe it's defective, boss." Quinton Cooper was a paramedic, or he had been before June 6th. Now he was her assistant fire chief.

"Maybe. Or maybe we're not big enough to warrant an answer. Regardless, no answer might be the best-case scenario."

"You're worried?"

"About that?" She tilted her head toward the gazebo and gave him a pointed glance.

"I know. I know." He held up his rather large hands and grinned at her. Quinton Cooper had a smile that could brighten the darkest of days. "You're worried about everything. I get it."

He'd probably been the last person to see her fiancé alive. They'd been making ambulance runs to Fort Stockton with folks injured from the train wreck in Alpine. That was the last anyone had seen or heard of Hunter Johns, but the picture Quinton had painted of Fort Stockton hadn't been a rosy one. In all likelihood, Hunter had not survived. It was the not knowing that bothered Dixie the most.

"Why isn't anyone watching the box?" Quinton asked.

"I was. We are."

He laughed. "Whose shift is it?"

"Ezekiel."

"Good man."

"That he is. I told him to take a break, get some water, that I didn't mind subbing in for a few minutes."

The Council had decided that someone would stay with the box in the gazebo in case it emitted some sort of signal. Shifts were divided into three-hour slots. Folks showed up faithfully for their shift. Dixie found herself walking past it even when the gazebo was not on her route. She didn't mind a few extra steps. She barely noticed. Her life consisted of walking from one place to the other, or, if she was lucky, using one of the horses.

Ezekiel returned and thanked her, and she and Quinton headed over to see what could be salvaged from a barn that had gone up in flames the week before. Lightning had caused the initial fire. It had been completely engulfed before they even arrived. Such was life as a firefighter in Alpine Texas. They'd been fortunate that it hadn't spread to the nearby residence.

She walked by the gazebo again that evening, and twice the next day.

What did she think she'd see?

What was she hoping for?

After forty-eight hours of no response, the Council decided the beacon could be moved to the police station. Folks were welcome to stop by and take a peek at it whenever they had the urge. They could stare at it, examine it, even pray over the device. Dixie tried to resist going in to gaze at it because she knew that Tanda had enough on her shoulders without hosting a continuous crowd of lookie-loos.

A few more days slipped by, and the beacon became less of an object of interest. If not forgotten, it ceased to be a priority. The June heat slammed into them with the force of a passenger train sideswiping a freight train, reminding Dixie of the remnants of the two trains that had collided in Alpine on the morning the satellites fell. The wreckage had never been moved. How would it? The bodies had been buried. Those still alive rendered aid. The cars emptied of anything that might be useful, but the wreckage remained—a constant reminder of that fateful day.

And in Alpine, one year and five days after that tragic event, they waited to see if the beacon would bring help to their town. Everyone appeared to be consumed with the exhausting task of simply trying to survive.

Dixie was left wondering if she was stuck in some macabre, apocalyptic version of Ground Hog Day. Nothing changed. Nothing improved, and the summer stretched out before them like the blacktop highways that led away from Alpine.

Was anyone still out there?

And if they were, would they be friend or foe?

CHAPTER 6

Tanda and Dixie sat on the front porch of Perry Reed's house, or the house that had been assigned to him. They didn't have a housing shortage in Alpine. Their population drop had left many empty buildings and homes. Some people had packed up and left in the first few days. Others had tried to stick it out and succumbed to sickness or died in one of the battles they'd been forced to wage. Still others made it through the winter but left in search of family once spring arrived.

"Explain it to us again," Tanda said.

"Not a lot to explain."

"But you've worked the odds over in your mind." Dixie was sitting with her back to the afternoon sun.

Perry squinted at her—either because of the light or maybe because he was trying to formulate his thoughts.

"If you want a scientific answer—a technical answer—then sure. I've done the calculations."

"Calculations?" Tanda glanced at Dixie, then back toward Perry.

"Probability. In my opinion, there's a better than 95% chance that the beacon did work. The bigger question is whether anybody is still waiting on the other end."

"They can't all be dead." Dixie's voice sounded grim to her own ears, and she realized that a small part of her feared that very thing might be true. "The whole world can't be dead."

"Only a few would have had access to the receiver—Isaac Thornfield or one of his people."

"His people." Tanda shook her head in disbelief. "You think they would have stayed with him? Even after all that happened?"

"I do. Most would have. Thornfield would have picked people without family, upping the odds of their staying. He also would have enough provisions to keep them well-fed. Thornfield thought things through. The man was a master of contingency plans."

"Okay." Tanda nodded. "So if Thornfield or his people survived, why hasn't anyone answered?"

It had been five days since they'd activated the beacon. Dixie thought Tanda looked ready to jump out of her skin. Plainly, she had thought something would happen. The fact that nothing at all had occurred only made her all the more twitchy. She'd come in search of Dixie at lunch and asked her to come on a "fact-finding mission."

"The question those on the receiving end will be asking is simple," Perry explained. "Who activated it? If Thornfield believes one of the people in the habitat did so, he'll show—eventually. But he'll plainly see the device was activated in Alpine, which could mean it's in the hands of people who aren't loyal to him. In that case, he might choose to ignore it."

"Wait." Dixie stood, paced the length of the small porch, then stopped abruptly in front of Perry and Tanda. "If most, or all, of the lower orbital satellites fell, how would he have the ability to know where the beacon's signal originated from? How would he have any GPS tracking ability?"

For his answer, Perry pointed a single finger to the sky.

"I don't get it," Tanda admitted.

"Most of the commercial satellites were in the lower orbit, but GPS is mid-orbit."

"Seriously?" Tanda looked puzzled. "The first day of the fall, after the train had crashed, our station was full of people whose GPS no longer worked."

"A GPS system on a car or a mobile phone works by receiving radio signals from one of the GPS satellites, which depends on a direct path. That path was obscured during the cataclysmic collapse of the lower satellites, but I suspect they're working again now. The debris field is, no doubt, beginning to clear. It won't be a consistent signal, but it will work from time to time."

"Okay. So Thornfield will know the beacon was activated in Alpine." Dixie was having trouble wrapping her mind around the idea that anyone still had usable technology. "If the GPS satellites are still functional."

"Remember, Thornfield isn't just another rich guy. He's not only in the top one percent—"

"I doubt that term applies anymore," Tanda muttered.

"I assure you it does. Thornfield was in the top one percent of the one percent. Most of the people who were in that category had contingency plans for a scenario like we're living through. They'll have shelters, bunkers, even medical facilities. And they'll have a large stash of supplies."

"What kind of supplies?" Tanda narrowed her eyes and crossed her arms.

"Everything we don't have—medicine, ammunition, food, clean water, even precious metals."

"Gold? They have gold in their bunkers?"

Perry smiled and shrugged his shoulders. "Probably. It's called diversifying, and you can bet the people we're talking about did. You can also be sure that Thornfield had a backup plan."

"What kind of backup plan?" Dixie sat, elbows on her knees, studying the man.

"Contingencies. Remember? He would have satellites in mid or high orbit, and those would probably—to some extent—still work. The problem would be the lack of infrastructure on the ground. But the box? It would activate a signal, bounce off the upper satellite, and land in Thornfield's lap. He knows where. He knows when. He doesn't know who."

"Hence, the delay." Tanda ran a hand up and around the back of her neck.

"With Thornfield, basic calculations take on an entirely different slant. He never did anything unless it furthered his agenda, and for the last 10 years, his agenda had been getting humanity to Mars. That was the reason my team was locked in the dome to begin with."

Dixie froze, allowing her thoughts to run over the story of how Liam and Felicity had found them just minutes before their oxygen supply ran out. "Do you think he knew about the oxygen malfunction?"

"Yes. I suspect he did."

"Why wouldn't he..." Her words drifted away.

"Come and save us? Go back to calculations—the odds of arriving in time would have been low. The odds that we were still alive, lower still. It wasn't worth the risk. If Felicia and Liam hadn't found us, we would have died." He stopped speaking but continued to drum his fingers against the arm of the chair. "If this woman—Tía—hadn't sent them to us, I wouldn't be sitting here puzzling over this question. I still don't understand how any of that was possible."

Tía was an old woman who had taken on the role of spiritual leader in the Barrio where Cade and Harper had first sought refuge. El Paso had fallen pretty quickly, but the group of survivors in the Barrio had survived, largely due to Tía's leadership. She apparently had some sort of ability to see and know things that she shouldn't have been able to see or know. She'd given Liam and Felicia general directions and told them to look for a yellow door past the place where the cowboys played. Liam was former military. Felicia had been working at the McDonald Observatory when it had been attacked. She'd been the sole survivor and that had left a mark on her emotionally. The events of the last year had left her with an unusual ability to perceive things most people couldn't. Second sight? That's what Tanda called it. Dixie wasn't so sure. She suspected a concussion or injury had somehow changed Felicia's brain.

She couldn't make much sense of Tía or Felicia. But the fact remained that Liam and Felicia had found the biodome, behind the yellow door, past the old rodeo arena. They had rescued Perry and his crew mere minutes before their oxygen would have run out.

"I'm a man of science," Perry said. "I don't believe in old ladies who have visions or young women who dream dreams. But I've experienced what Felicia can do more than once, and I can't simply ignore those experiences. As a scientist, it's something my mind is still grappling with."

"Why didn't you use the beacon in the biodome?" Tanda was sitting back now, thoughtfully studying him.

Dixie had seen that expression on her friend's face many times—a strained sense of calm.

"The beacon's purpose was to call Thornfield when the test was over. It didn't work inside the dome. The dome was built with a sort of shield around it—a life-size Faraday cage, if you will. Nothing in. Nothing out. It was critical that we knew we were on our own. Otherwise, it wouldn't authentically represent a journey to Mars."

Dixie was shaking her head before he'd finished. Tanda was muttering something about the gall of the super-rich, which was probably what spurred Perry to try again.

"I didn't use the beacon then because I knew it wouldn't work inside the biodome. Isolation was the purpose of the exercise. Could we survive? To Thornfield, our survival was merely an experiment, albeit a very important experiment. If everything had gone as planned, the biodome doors would've opened just past the one-year mark—the twelve month anniversary of the day we went in. Only at that point would Thornfield have expected my team to activate the beacon. So, I end where I began. There's a 95% chance that Thornfield will come. Not for humanitarian reasons. But to check on his experiment."

"Thank you for walking us through it," Tanda said.

Dixie added, "We both were present when you explained it to the Council. We just needed to hear it again."

Perry nodded in understanding. "They listened, questioned, and ultimately decided it was worth the risk. The people of your town rescued me and my crew. You also gave us refuge. It seemed only fitting that your Council should be the ones to decide whether to activate the beacon."

Tanda stood, shook his hand, then walked down the porch and waited for Dixie.

"I've been here in Alpine less than three months," Perry said. "Already I understand that the people here are vastly different than the man that I worked for."

Dixie followed his gaze to Tanda, who was staring off at the mountains as if she could see what might be about to happen.

"True," Dixie said. "What I've learned is that Tanda, the Council—really all of the people remaining here—will go to any length to protect and support one another."

"That's a rare thing," Perry said.

"Yeah. I get that, but it's only as a group that we have any chance of survival. You're part of that group now."

"I know it."

"We're glad you're here... you and your team."

Dixie walked back to the center of town with Tanda. They parted ways at the police station having accomplished very little. More than that, Tanda's restless energy had been contagious. Dixie's mood resembled the air before a thunderstorm. Something was about to happen. The question was whether any of them would be left standing when it did.

LATER THAT AFTERNOON, Tanda related the entire conversation to Liam, who stopped by to update her on what their scouting party had observed to the northeast. His first question on entering her office was, "Anything from the beacon?"

"Nothing." She explained Perry's theory, then said, "Tell me what you saw."

"Seems to be a build-up of some kind." He sank into the chair across from her and accepted the cup of water, downed it, then passed the cup back. Liam was former military, thirty-two years old, tall and fit, with long hair pulled back and a bushy beard that he'd recently trimmed.

"Did they look like military?"

"Maybe. Honestly, we didn't get that close. If I can see them, then you can bet they can see me. We stayed a safe distance back."

"So you saw what? Exactly?"

"Vehicles. Several of them. Reflections which might also indicate weapons or tent poles."

"But why would anyone take up residence in such an isolated location... You're sure this was south of Stockton?"

"Yup."

"There's nothing out there but desert."

"Logan says there's an old ranching compound that direction."

Tanda stared at the framed county map on her wall. "I'd forgotten about that. Place is—was—owned by an old rancher named Gutterson."

"Survivalist?"

"Matt Gutterson wouldn't have used that term, but yeah. Pretty much."

"Has anyone seen or heard from him in the last year?"

Tanda shook her head, trying to remember. "He stopped in town a couple of times after June 6th. I think he came once a month to purchase what he couldn't grow or make on his own. Basic supplies. He always had something to trade for what he needed. I spoke to him once about moving into town and he nearly laughed, which would have floored me. I've barely seen the old guy smile."

She knew that she couldn't check on every rancher in the county, but how was it that she hadn't noticed the absence of Gutterson? "Crotchety old guy. Wife passed years ago. Kids moved off to the city."

"My guess is they—whoever *they* are—have opted to use his place as a base."

"Can't see Gutterson going for that."

"Then he either fled or they killed him."

"Okay." Tanda rubbed her eyes. "I should share this with the Council so we can send out a message to neighborhood liaisons."

"The Council meeting is at six tonight." He grinned at her when she tossed him an exasperated look. "I knew that's what you'd say."

"Why stop by and update me personally then?"

"You deserve to hear it firsthand, boss."

"I'm not your boss."

"You're not *not* my boss."

"That makes no sense."

To which Liam snapped off a salute. She liked Liam Contreras, even if he had been on the wrong side of things a year ago.

"Back to the beacon" Liam interlaced his fingers behind his head and stared up at the corner of her ceiling. "Does Perry have any idea where this Thornfield character might have been in the last twelve months?"

"Best guess—one of his bunkers."

"He has bunkers? Plural?" Liam wiggled his eyes. "A private bunker or one of the government bunkers?"

"Probably his choice. I suspect his private bunker would have more amenities."

"Yeah, those government places like Raven Rock and Mount Weather were supposedly pretty barebones. Some didn't even have cots—just sleeping bags."

"Sleeping bags? For the military?"

"We've endured worse."

"I never gave government bunkers much thought." Tanda shifted in her chair. She needed to get home, eat something, clean up for the meeting. "I'd heard of them, sure, but it's kind of hard to swallow the concept. You're positive there are such places and that it isn't just an..." She waved toward the empty street beyond her window. "Urban myth."

"Not a myth. I was pretty low in the military command structure, but even I heard rumors of COG."

"COG means Continuity of Government?"

"Exactly."

"Watched a Netflix special on that once. At the time, it seemed a bit—overdramatized."

"And now?"

Tanda shook her head, unwilling to go there. Did she wish she'd been better prepared? Sure. Even if she had known what would happen on June 6th, would she have joined the prepper side of the equation? No. Her job was here, in the middle of Alpine. Not in a bunker several hundred feet underground. Not with Thornfield. Not even on Gutterson's ranch.

"I don't see Thornfield spending the last twelve months underground with a bunch of government workers eating MREs." Liam stretched his arms up and back, causing his spine to emit popping sounds.

"You think Thornfield knew what was happening."

"I do," Liam admitted. "It's the reason he accelerated the timeline for the biodome. I've talked to the entire group about this—Nan, Perry, Kenneth, and Aisha. They were alerted in the middle of the night on the 5th—before the morning when the trains crashed here. They made their way to Van Horn, where they spent forty-eight hours in quarantine, then entered the biodome."

"Quarantining from what?"

"Kenneth said it was standard operating procedure."

"More likely, Thornfield was sending the rest of the workers home."

"Wouldn't want anyone tipping off the Orion crew that something calamitous had happened. If they had known that civilization was disintegrating, they might have reconsidered a twelve-month stay in the dome."

"You're probably right." Tanda felt irritated and nervously energetic, as if her body were preparing for a fight her mind hadn't yet recognized. "Thornfield was in front of this thing. He had to be."

"He put his crew in the biodome, knowing that they might not survive, and if they did survive, they'd come out to a world they no longer recognized."

"Probably made the experiment all the more on point. Think about it, Liam. If Thornfield knew the satellites were down and society—worldwide—was on the edge of collapse, it would have given him a nearly perfect scenario. No way to cheat. No one to sneak pizza to the people inside. No way for them to receive letters from their family. He tried to create an experiment that would determine whether a handful of people, a small group of scientists, could survive in a small space for an extended period of time. The fall of the satellites was the perfect scenario."

They stared at one another a few seconds, then both shrugged. There was so much they didn't know in this new world, and they were slowly learning to accept that. They might never know. You gathered the information you could find, and you made your decisions accordingly.

Tanda walked with Liam out through the receptionist space, nodding at Edna who was turning things over to Stu Avery.

"All good?" Tanda asked.

"Yup."

All four of them eyed the box, but no one bothered asking. It was plain as the sun setting in the west that the box had no information to give them. Tanda went home, washed up as best she could, donned a somewhat clean uniform, then headed to the Council meeting, which always took place at the Sul Ross campus.

The meeting went pretty much like Tanda thought it would. They were cautiously concerned. Groups had moved around Alpine before—some with ill intent, some just traveling from one part of the state to another.

They'd learned to be prepared but not overreact.

In all likelihood, the people camping to the north of town thought Alpine was deserted, like most other towns in West Texas. But if that was true, why had they stopped in the middle of nowhere? And what had happened to Gutterson? Maybe the old man had died in his sleep.

What the Council didn't want to do was draw attention to themselves. This wasn't about the beacon—at least no one gathered that night thought it was. There wasn't necessarily a cause-and-effect relationship between their activating the beacon and the arrival of the group to the north. Correlation did not always imply causation.

They would know soon enough if the group was something they would have to actively defend against. In the meantime, they'd distribute what ammunition remained, double patrols, and hope for the best.

As Tanda trudged to her apartment, the warning voice in her head kept insisting that the best rarely happened.

CHAPTER 7

Dixie couldn't let it go. The idea that Isaac Thornfield would have funded such a massive experiment, only to let the participants die? That notion was hard to swallow.

She went in search of Aisha Nkosi the next afternoon. Aisha had been part of the Orion crew. She'd been locked inside the biodome. When Liam and Felicia had freed the crew, Aisha had gone to search for her parents in her hometown of Pecos. Finding only a deserted house within a deserted town, she'd returned to Alpine.

Aisha was an emergency medicine physician. Alpine was fortunate to have two doctors—Miles and Cade—plus one vet, Logan. Upon Aisha's return, Logan had joked that he'd be able to get back to his first love—animals. But things hadn't worked out that way. Influenza hit hard during the winter months, followed by one medical emergency after another during the spring.

"Where do I think Thornfield has ridden out the last 12

months?" Aisha had opted to live in a small duplex that shared a wall with Dixie.

They'd become fast friends.

As they did most evenings, they sat on the front porch of their duplex, watching neighborhood kids play ball in the middle of the street.

Dixie would have walked a mile for a cold beer.

Even a glass of iced tea.

Instead, they sipped occasionally from bottles that had been filled with fresh rainwater.

"I think he probably had several escape plans," Aisha admitted. "Looking back, I think he understood that something like what happened–the Kessler Effect or another event equally destructive—was bound to occur. And if he knew that, then he had places to go. Probably several."

"So he just waited it out like the rest of us?"

"Doubtful." Aisha attempted a laugh that fell flat.

They were both exhausted. They were always exhausted. Dixie couldn't remember what it felt like to not be exhausted.

"My guess is his escape position was well funded, well-staffed, and well supplied."

"So he just goes in his bunker and what? Waits to hear from his group? Wouldn't he at least have come to Van Horn to check on you?"

"Nah. One thing I'm fairly sure about is that we weren't the only ones Thornfield hustled into a biodome as the satellite grid collapsed. You don't run a single experiment in isolation. You run several experiments with minor differences, but differences that are big enough to affect the possibility of a positive outcome."

Dixie cocked her head, her attention suddenly and completely focused on her friend. "You're saying he wouldn't put all of his eggs in one basket?"

"A valid analogy except he doesn't deal with eggs. He deals with people. And they are disposable in light of the greater mission."

"Sounds like a swell guy to work for."

"Isaac Thornfield paid well, easily double what anyone else offered. And he was doing cutting-edge research. He was years ahead of what our government was planning to do as far as interplanetary research and travel. So yeah, it was a sweet deal at the time."

Dixie hadn't really had girlfriends before June 6th. Of course, she and Tanda were friendly, but life had been busy then. They'd never socialized more than the occasional beer after a City Council meeting. All that had changed when they'd entered the postmodern era. Now Tanda was like her sister, and this woman—Aisha—was her best friend. Because of that, she didn't hesitate to ask, "Do you regret going into the biodome?"

"I'm not sure I'd say that I regret it. I wish I had not been so entirely focused on the mission. If I had maintained a broader perspective, I might've been able to prepare better. I might have seen what was coming." She sipped again from the water bottle and added with a grim expression, "I might have been able to prepare my parents."

"You don't know they're dead."

"And you don't know that Hunter is dead." Aisha's voice was soft, compassionate. "We may never know. For me, that's probably the hardest part."

"We still get up every day. Do what has to be done." Dixie hated the way that sounded. Old. It sounded old. She sounded old.

"That's what you do during an apocalypse." Aisha wiggled her eyebrows.

She was small with hair the color of obsidian stone. At least that's what that particular shade of black reminded Dixie of. Obsidian stone. It even had an exotic ring to it. Dixie had found one on vacation with her parents years ago, when they toured a volcanic site. She wondered what had happened to it. Still on the shelf in her childhood home? Was her childhood home still standing?

Aisha interrupted her trip down memory lane. "Do you ever feel ready to date again?"

Dixie had picked up her bottle of water and tilted her head back. The water hit her throat at the same moment that Aisha's words hit her ears. She spewed it on the concrete at her feet.

"Wasn't that crazy of an idea," Aisha said.

"It kind of was."

"Why?" And now Aisha's voice had grown even more serious. "You're a good-looking woman, Dixie. You need to live your life. Hunter, from what you've told me, would want that."

"Okay. Sure. You're right but for one thing." Now she sat back and smiled at her friend. "Who would I date? Last I checked all the dating sites are down."

"Which I consider a good thing—never was one for swiping left or right. Still, there are a few bachelors here in Alpine."

"The men you're talking about I've known all my life. Trying to start a relationship with them wouldn't work."

"What about Miles?"

"Huh-uh. He's more your type."

"My type?"

"You're both doctors."

"I have to date doctors?"

"I see how it is. You can dish it out, but you can't—"

"Oh, I can take it." Aisha laughed.

Dixie stood and stretched. She was feeling exhausted and

restless. How could she feel both things at the same time? "Want to walk over to Sul Ross?"

"Now?"

"Sure. Why not? It's not like we can go inside and watch the latest episode of *Survivor*."

"Did you watch *Survivor*?"

"Everyone watched *Survivor*. That and *Naked and Afraid*."

"Eww."

As they walked to the campus, their conversation shifted to more serious matters. Dixie explained that Perry often took patrol shifts with Liam. He and Liam seemed to have developed a comfortable friendship, though Perry was old enough to be Liam's father.

"Not sure Perry can tell you anything more about Thornfield than I have. And didn't you say you met with him earlier today?"

"Yeah. You're probably right. I just feel... itchy."

They arrived at the Sul Ross campus as Liam and Perry were unharnessing their mounts.

"Have a good ride?" Dixie asked.

"Yup." Liam tended to answer in one-word replies.

Dixie was certain that he knew it irritated her and did it intentionally. She was about to call him on it when Perry spoke up.

"Encampment to the north hasn't moved. Nothing else to report."

"Any ideas who it might be?" Dixie asked, directing the question to Liam, wondering how she could provoke him into speaking full sentences.

"None."

"So they're still there?"

"Yup."

"Any idea why they're holed up there?"

"None." Liam grinned at Dixie.

She wanted to punch him. She hadn't wanted to punch a guy since her first crush in junior high. Aisha's question came back to her. Was she ready to date? Did she have a crush on Liam Contreras? Wasn't he dating Felicia?

Perry seemed to notice some sort of nonverbal tennis match was going on between Dixie and Liam. He shook his head in amusement at the two of them. "Since the Council doesn't want us approaching, there's not much to do but keep an eye on them, make sure they're not coming closer, and wait."

He seemed about to go on when there was a commotion at the entrance to the livestock area and then Felicia dashed up to where they were standing. She bent over, her long auburn hair falling around her face. Hands on thighs, she sucked in huge gulps of air.

"Take it easy," Aisha said. "You're going to hyper-ventilate."

"What's wrong?" Liam asked.

Felicia held up a finger.

Dixie shifted her weight from one foot to another as she said, "Take your time," but actually meant, "For the love of God tell us."

Felicia nodded then stood up straight, her gaze moving from Liam to Perry, then Aisha, then Dixie. "Someone's coming."

TANDA HEARD IT FROM LOGAN, who was alerted to the situation by one of his interns banging on his apartment door.

"We have a plan for this," he reminded her as she dressed and strapped on her gun belt.

"And we can hope that people will follow it. Are you coming with—"

"Yup."

They'd only been a couple for two months. Tanda hadn't even realized she cared for him until he'd nearly bled to death at the Marathon Hotel. At that moment, she realized how empty her life would be without him. She had been more frightened than she'd ever been in her life. She'd felt a level of grief that she hadn't even realized it was possible to feel.

Logan Wright was her oldest friend. Her best friend.

She paused, reached up, touched his face, then ran her fingers through his hair that she'd recently cut at his insistence. She'd done a terrible job.

"Let's go," she said grimly.

They hurried from Logan's apartment down to the corral area where Liam and Perry were already saddling two mounts.

"Be careful," Liam said, tossing her Roxy's reins.

Perry walked Aurora over to Logan. "She's rested," he said, and Logan swung up in the saddle.

Tanda hesitated for only a second, then said, "We need you both with us."

Two other interns brought fresh mounts to Liam and Perry.

Dixie assured her that she'd help notify neighborhood coordinators.

"And I'll get things ready in the medical center," Aisha said. "Just in case."

As the four of them rode out of town, Tanda told herself they were ready. They had a plan for nearly every contingency. But a plane landing at the local airport? If they had a plan for that, she couldn't remember the exact details. Honestly, she hadn't given much thought to someone arriving by air, even after activating the beacon.

But she trusted that the people of Alpine had changed

since June 6th of the year before. They understood that every potentially threatening event brought consequences. They had agreed to a defensive plan, and now they would stick to it. She saw evidence of as much as they rode toward the airport. Mothers hustled children inside. Men and women joined those on patrol to assume defensive positions that formed a perimeter around the town. People looked serious and a little scared, but they called out "Godspeed" and "Stay safe" and even "Give 'em hell, if you have to."

It was less than three miles from the university to the municipal airport, which hadn't seen much activity in the last year. OK, it hadn't seen any activity. There had been a time when Tanda had wondered about that. Surely some people had planes and tanks filled with jet fuel. But none of those people chose to come to Alpine. No one arrived to offer assistance. During that first horrific week, they'd sometimes heard planes overhead, always so high that they'd been imperceptible to the naked eye. Somehow, she had forgotten that the airport even existed. Now she, Logan, Perry, and Liam rode toward it at a fast canter. They were still a fair distance from the landing field when the setting sun glinted off a plane's wings.

Liam paused to look through his binoculars, then spurred his mare to catch up with them. "It's a Cessna."

Perry added, "Probably Thornfield's."

They picked up the pace so that it seemed to Tanda that they were galloping toward their future, then abruptly stopped at some arbitrary line just short of the airfield. Tanda glassed the area, as did Liam. Tanda passed her binoculars to Logan. Liam gave his to Perry.

"Looks like a billionaire's plaything to me," Perry said. "But we're not close enough for me to make out the people."

"How about I go ahead?" Liam suggested.

But Tanda was already spurring her mount. "We do this together."

As they approached, it was easy enough to make out the three guards, but she didn't see anyone who looked like a billionaire. Two men and one woman dressed in black held military-grade rifles at the ready. They were pointed toward the ground, not toward the approaching party.

Tanda urged her mount into the lead, Logan and Perry followed, and Liam brought up the tail end of the group. They were a small welcome committee, which seemed as it should be since they didn't know if these people were friend or foe. She'd always imagined the Council as a whole greeting the first responders who would one day ride into Alpine. These folks did not look like they had flown in to offer aid. She was glad it was only the four of them representing Alpine. She wasn't willing to risk any additional lives.

The plane was a thing of beauty, boasting a white finish with a blue stripe down the side. The main entry door, which was open, was positioned between the cockpit and the wing. Six large oval-shaped windows were situated between the door and the engines.

"No number on the tail." Liam had caught up with her.

"Odd."

"And illegal."

How long had it been since she'd seen something shiny and new? How long had it been since she'd seen working transportation from the 21st century? And yet the guards around the plane acted as if this was something they did every day. Probably it was. When they were within 30 feet from the jet, one of the guards stepped forward and raised his hand in the universal halt gesture.

They stopped as if they were in formation—equal length apart, all facing the plane. Four delegates from Alpine, Texas.

The guard who had raised his hand stepped forward. "Identification?" His eyes were plainly focused on Perry.

Tanda realized this man had been alerted as to whom he might expect on the other end of that beacon call, though no doubt they were surprised to find that the call came from Alpine and not Van Horn where the beacon had been located.

"I don't have it on me," Perry said.

The guard's attention shifted across the group, took in their weapons, and then he moved his forefinger next to the trigger of the M4 Carbine—a shorter and lighter version of the M16A2 rifle. Tanda had trained on an M4 years ago, but it wasn't something Alpine had in their armory. In fact, the word *armory* was a stretch for their small cache of weapons.

The other guards had widened their position around the plane, no doubt worried about an attack from the other flanks.

"I have identification," Tanda said. "May I approach?"

The guard shook his head once—definitively. "You weren't on the list."

"And yet, without Tanda, who is the Chief of Police for the town of Alpine, I wouldn't be here." Perry shifted in his saddle. "Just tell Thornfield that we're here."

Before the situation could grow more tense, a man appeared in the open door at the top of the stairs of the jet. Even from a distance, Tanda could see that he wore designer clothes, designer sunglasses, even designer shoes. He did not look like he'd spent the last twelve months trying to survive the apocalypse. The man's voice, when he spoke, was low and authoritative.

"Let Perry pass."

But Perry was already shaking his head. "If they don't come, I don't come. And if I don't come, you will never know what happened to your little experiment."

The man standing in the doorway to the plane tilted his

head, apparently unaccustomed to having his commands questioned, but then he shrugged and said, "Very well. Please, Perry, you and your friends are welcome aboard."

Tanda wasn't about to put all four of them onboard that plane. "Liam and Logan, watch the horses and keep your eyes on these soldiers of fortune. They look twitchy to me." She glanced at Perry, indicating he should pass his horse's reins to Logan.

"We'll approach," she said to Perry, but in a voice loud enough for Thornfield to hear. "But let's do this out in the open."

Tanda imagined she could see the irritation in Thornfield's gaze, even behind his overly priced Gucci glasses. But either he was too tired or too impatient to argue with them. He walked down the stairs, motioned his guards away with a flick of his wrist, and waited for the group from Alpine to come closer.

Liam and Logan remained on their horses, but moved within ten yards of the plane, still holding the reins of Tanda's and Perry's horses. Tanda walked with Perry until they were close enough to shake hands with Thornfield, something he did not offer to do. She was comforted by the fact that she still had ammunition in her service revolver, and she would use it should any of Thornfield's guards prove dangerous. But she understood that she would at best get one or two shots off before she was mowed down by their superior weapons. Still, it gave her a measure of peace to know that she could and would defend those in her party.

As would Liam and Logan.

They'd all become fine shots over the last twelve months.

Even Perry had learned to shoot a rifle. He'd practiced with a pellet rifle. He didn't carry one because they didn't have one to give him.

Thornfield didn't waste any time. "How many of you survived?"

"The entire team."

"And they're here?"

"Some are."

Thornfield hesitated, glancing left and right. Finally, he said, "We're wheels up in twenty minutes. Go get them. We can debrief in flight."

"No."

It was an interesting thing for Tanda to watch. She'd seen her fair share of miscreants, maniacs, and outright villains in the last year. Thornfield was different. He was perhaps the most arrogant person she'd ever met, and she hadn't actually met him yet. Plainly, he issued commands that he expected would be followed. He was taken aback by Perry's "No."

"I don't understand."

"I'm not going with you. And I have no interest in debriefing you on a mission that would have killed the entire Orion crew if it weren't for Tanda's people rescuing us."

Thornfield's gaze flicked toward Tanda and immediately dismissed her.

"What do you want?"

"This isn't a negotiation."

"Everything's a negotiation." Thornfield glanced at his watch—a Rolex, of course.

"Late for a meeting, Isaac?"

Thornfield colored at the use of his given name. "As a matter of fact, I am. Now get your *team* and get on the *plane*, Perry. Whatever it is you *want* we can discuss, but I don't have time to *waste* on a dramatic reunion."

The guy apparently liked to emphasize certain words to make his point, as if he were talking to children. He was grating on Tanda's nerves, and she'd been quiet about as long as it was physically possible for her to be so.

"You heard him. He's not going with you, Thornfield. Neither are Kenneth Black, Aisha Nkosi, or Nan Cooper. As for Rajesh Patel, the last my team saw of him he was running out into the desert. Apparently, your little experiment drove him mad."

"My little experiment had a high statistical probability of saving humanity."

"I doubt that, Isaac." Perry shook his head as if disappointed in his old boss's lack of understanding. "You didn't figure in several things—including the human factor."

If ever a billionaire could look flustered, Thornfield did.

"Fine. You'd rather stay here and play *Fallout* in the real world. Go ahead and do that. I can see why you wouldn't want to go back to a gleaming lab with state-of-the-art equipment and the chance to get off this pitiful rock of a planet. Stay with your new friends, Perry. You suit one another."

Perry glanced at Tanda, who shrugged.

So Thornfield's plane hadn't turned out to be a golden chariot swooping in to save the people of Alpine. She hadn't actually expected it would be.

They turned and walked back toward Liam and Logan and had crossed half the distance when Isaac Thornfield called out, "I hope you're ready for what's coming your way."

Tanda and Perry stopped.

She looked at him, closed her eyes for a second, then they both turned and faced Thornfield.

"And what is that?" Perry asked.

"Not what. Who." Thornfield had jerked off his sunglasses, and he once again wore an expression of smug superiority. "The government has sent out one of their little expeditions.

They're setting up camp in Fort Davis right now, and you can bet they'll be swooping in to declare martial law any moment."

"You mean Stockton," Tanda said.

"What?"

"You said Fort Davis, but you meant Stockton."

"I meant Fort Davis." And then Thornfield turned and jogged up the flight of stairs.

By the time Tanda and Perry had rejoined Liam and Logan, the guards had boarded the plane and it was speeding down the runway. The Cessna lifted off, the landing gear retracted, and then it was no more than a speck in the dying light of another summer day.

"I'd forgotten they looked like that," Logan admitted.

"Assholes?"

"Planes."

"Ah."

"What did he want?" Liam asked. "Other than to reclaim his people."

"That was pretty much it." Perry's smile was pure, genuine, beautiful. "I must say I enjoyed telling him we weren't interested."

"All right, then." Logan settled into his saddle as they turned back toward Alpine. "Not here to save us, but neither were they here to take from us. Let's call it a draw."

"Not exactly." Tanda's mind was swirling with possibilities of what Thornfield's news might mean. None of them were good.

"Meaning?"

"The military's coming," Perry explained.

"That's who is camping out at the Gutterson Ranch?"

"Nope." Tanda shook her head. "According to Thornfield, the military is camped at Fort Davis."

"Then who is at Gutterson's?"

"A very good question."

And even more important than the *who* was the *why*. One way or another, Tanda was about to find out the answers to both questions.

CHAPTER 8

The Council met that evening.

Tanda briefed everyone on what Thornfield had said and they again discussed Liam's previous update on the group to the north. "Basically we have two probably unrelated situations. My recommendation is that we deal with both immediately."

"I agree," Harper said. "It no longer seems wise to lie low."

The fact that she was holding seven-week-old Kai was a testament to the fact that she had as much or more to lose than anyone in the room. The baby girl slept peacefully in her arms, unaware of the urgency in the people around her.

"Ignoring problems rarely works," Tanda agreed. "Hoping for the best—well, that isn't enough in this instance. We need to find out who these two groups are and what they want."

"Which is inherently risky." Keme held up his hands to ward off his sister's reply. "I'm not saying we shouldn't do it, Tanda. I'm only saying we will be taking a chance."

"Getting out of bed every morning entails taking a chance,"

Gonzo said. As the representative of the artist community that had been in place in the area before the satellites fell, Gonzo often had a unique perspective on things. "In fact, doing nothing is taking a chance. I agree with Tanda and Harper. It's better to know what we're facing."

"I propose we send out two parties. One to Gutterson's Ranch. The other to Fort Davis. Any volunteers?" Tanda was surprised when Dixie held up her hand. "You're sure?"

"I haven't been out of Alpine since this thing began, and I'm feeling a little restless. I wouldn't mind going to Fort Davis. Aisha could go with me. She knows the lay of the land in that direction."

"I'd rather Aisha stay here." Logan looked apologetic as he said it. "We have two more babies due soon and three folks still at the Maverick Inn in recovery from minor surgery. Plus we need to make house calls for those who can't get in to see me or Miles or Cade or Aisha. I know with four doctors now it sounds as if we could handle it, but I also have animals calving. I'd rather Aisha stay."

"I'll go," Keme said. "I can go with Tanda. Liam can go with Dixie."

Tanda knew her parents wouldn't like it. They were understanding of what she and Keme had done to help the people of Alpine. They had even supported her in the spring when she'd gone south in search of food and a trade route. Since the satellites fell, they'd largely stayed on their small acreage outside of town. They wouldn't be happy to have both of their children—albeit *adult* children—leave on a fact-finding mission. But they would accept that it made sense.

As did the Council.

The vote was unanimous in favor of making contact with both groups. The meeting broke up. Logan touched her arm, said he needed to check on a patient and that he'd see her back at the campus later.

Ron Mullins walked over to her. "When will you leave?"

"First light."

"And you're sure two per party is enough?"

Tanda put a hand on his shoulder. "Two per party is perfect. We can move fast, respond quickly to any threat, and get back swiftly with any information."

He nodded, then surprised her by enfolding her in a hug. Tanda had never been a touchy type of person, but she was learning to show affection while you had the chance because it might be the last chance you had. She patted his back, then motioned for Dixie, Liam, and Keme to follow her outside.

Sul Ross was situated on a rise at the edge of town. From there, the view was amazing. And with the absence of artificial light, the stars were putting on quite a show. A large moon had risen in the east, providing enough light for them to see one another, or at least the shadows of one another.

Tanda turned to face Keme, Liam, and Dixie. "First, are we sure about our teams?"

"Meaning what?" Keme had changed more than any other person she knew. The collapse of the modern world wasn't the cause of that transformation, but rather the death of his wife in their first major battle with Marfa. Lucy had given her life for the town of Alpine, for them, and she wasn't sure that Keme would ever recover from that.

"Maybe Liam should go with me, and you should go with Dixie."

"I don't think so." Liam shrugged when they all turned to stare at him. "Thornfield said the military is at Fort Davis."

"Doesn't mean it's true. I am the one who suggested we check it out, but that doesn't mean I believe him. I don't even know the man."

"Okay. But for a moment let's assume that he was telling the truth."

"Billionaires don't really need to make an impression by lying," Dixie added.

Liam nodded in agreement. "It's also true that a military unit camping in Fort Davis doesn't make a lot of sense. We all know there's nothing out that way."

"Wasn't very much there before June 6th," Dixie agreed.

"I can think of no strategic reason for them to position a team there now."

"You were in the military," Tanda reminded him. "There must be a reason if they are, in fact, there."

"My first reaction on hearing Thornfield say the government was at the fort was that he was wrong. Maybe he received some bad information. Maybe he was lying to mess with us."

"Dixie's probably right on that point," Tanda said. "I can't think of any motive he might have to lie. It seemed to me that he was almost gleeful when he said it. Hadn't put on his stupid sunglasses yet, and it was as if I could see a little spark in his evil eyes. He wasn't happy that Perry had turned him down. When he told us about Fort Davis, it felt like a sort of afterthought. As for the information being wrong, Thornfield would probably chop off the head of anyone who gave him bad information."

Keme sank back against the brick building. "So at the very least, he believes it to be true."

"As Tanda said, doesn't make it true." Dixie crossed her arms and waited. "What are you thinking, Liam?"

"That they're more than likely a group trying to appear to be the military."

"Again, though..." Tanda rubbed at a knot forming in the back of her neck. "Why?"

"Hopefully we'll find out. I can recognize whether a group is military or not. You can't fake that—not to someone who has been on the inside."

"Okay. And the people between here and Fort Stockton?"

"Never claimed to be military. Maybe they're a traveling group settling down for a few weeks, and then they'll press on. Or maybe they heard we have a comparatively good thing going on here and they want it."

"It's been several days." Keme's voice had grown hard. "They should have sent a scout to us by now."

"They have to know we're watching them," Liam agreed.

Then Dixie voiced the thing that had been bothering Tanda. "What are the odds that both groups would arrive at the same time?"

"Low. Nil, maybe." Tanda suddenly realized she needed sleep and needed it badly. Sunrise would come early, and she still had to pack. But hurrying this... That wasn't wise either. "How will you be able to tell, Liam? How will you know if they're the military or merely someone pretending to be the military?"

"It's safe to assume that a legitimate military group would be well supplied—transportation, weapons, lots of gear and food and fuel. They'll have it all. I'd expect a contingency of a hundred people, maybe more. They'll have a distinct chain of command, and they'll have a specific mission. They'll be here for a reason."

Tanda digested what he'd said, tried to lock it into her memory. Just in case the group between them and Fort Stockton claimed to be military. Just in case she had to figure out if that was true. "That all makes sense. Okay. Let's keep the teams as they are. Dixie and Liam, you're traveling twenty-four miles, which is an easy day's ride on horseback."

"Three days total." Dixie sounded eager, ready. "One day

there, one day so Liam can get the lay of the land, one day back."

"We should be back sooner than that," Keme said.

Tanda couldn't resist the urge to say, "Only initiate contact if it seems wise to do so."

Neither Liam nor Dixie bothered to answer that.

"I'm stating the obvious," Tanda muttered.

"That's okay, sis." Keme's tone, for a moment, lightened. "We've all learned to let you do that. Helps with your disposition."

"Seriously, Keme?"

He put his arm around her and pulled her close.

She thought he might give her a noogie, but he only grinned and dropped his arms after planting a kiss on her head. They weren't even out of town and already his mood was improving. Maybe this was exactly what her brother needed.

"Do you remember where the Gutterson Ranch is?" Liam teased.

"I have a map, but yeah, I remember."

"I suggest you circle around and approach from the north-west. They'll be watching Highway 67."

"Yup."

Tanda expected Keme and Liam to shake on it. Instead, all four of them formed a kind of huddle, an Alpine Huddle, heads touching, arms around one another, hearts beating in rhythm as one.

Or so it seemed.

Tanda went back to her apartment long enough to pack. Looking around the place, she wondered why she insisted on still calling it home. It wasn't. Logan's place was home. His ridiculous apartment on the Sul Ross campus was where she wanted to be. It was half the size of her place, but the amount of space she had didn't matter. Even the things she owned didn't matter—at least, most of it didn't.

She looked around the apartment—at the vertical blinds, digital television, breakfast nook, and upgraded appliances. She'd felt like a grown-up when she'd signed the lease. Having been newly appointed as Alpine's chief of police, she'd considered the move a step up. She'd told herself she'd commit to a house with a two-car garage in five years—seven at the most.

Zipping her bag closed, she walked out of the apartment. There was no need to lock it. Half of the units were empty, and the other half were filled with people she worked beside every day. She walked down the deserted streets of Alpine, her mind still snagging on the difference between then and now. On the difference in her.

She knew her own mind better.

Understood what things mattered.

Understood what things didn't.

As she climbed the hill to the Sul Ross campus, she felt something akin to happiness. Not over what would happen the next day or the day after that. But happiness that she was making her way toward someone she cared about and someone who cared about her. Tanda spent the evening lying in Logan's arms. She tried to memorize the smell and feel of him. Tried to place a marker on the memory of this night.

Which was overly dramatic, even for her.

Was her instinct telling her to expect trouble to the north? She'd learned to expect trouble every day. How would a few people gathered on a small deserted ranch be any different? How could they possibly be any worse than the miscreants and outlaws and insurgents she'd dealt with in the past year?

This was a fact-finding mission, pure and simple. Keme would have her back and she'd have his. Perhaps they'd approach. Maybe they'd just watch. Regardless, she'd be back in Alpine in twenty-four hours. Forty-eight at the most.

As long as one of their horses didn't step in a hole.

Or get bitten by a rattlesnake.

As long as they didn't encounter any other desperados, meandering through the desert. Summer was upon them, and the heat should cause people to hunker down. But sometimes it meant people grew more aggressive.

She had packed her firearm and extra ammunition.

Keme would have his bow and a quiver full of arrows.

His bow and arrows. She sighed as the full weight of that settled on her. Some days it still startled her how quickly they'd fallen back into the old ways.

Tanda thought she might toss and turn going over all the things that could go wrong. She didn't. Instead, she fell into a deep, dreamless sleep. Something told her she was going to need it.

EVERY EVENING, after the sun had slipped below the horizon, Gus met with Aimee and Sorrell outside on the old wood-slatted porch. It felt natural to call Aimee by her given name. But with Sorrell it was different. Gus suspected the man's own mother called him by his last name.

The three made a solid leadership group for the team, which had dropped from twenty to seventeen given the three who had been killed in confrontations on the journey to Texas. Aimee dealt with personnel. Sorrell handled security. As for Gus, he focused on what he'd come there to do. Implement the New World Map. Make adjustments to the model. Report back to Major Lawrence, who would report to General Kendricks.

Any hesitation over roles had fled somewhere in East

Texas. They'd accepted him as the *de facto* leader of their small group. He had accepted them as the defenders, and Gus understood that without them this plan wouldn't be possible at all. The world—literally—had gone too far. It was part of the reason that the regional centers were so important. They had to re-establish law and order. They had to regain the people's trust.

"Why are you opposed to sending out a scout party?" Aimee asked. It wasn't the first time she'd floated this idea. She had been in favor of going straight to Alpine.

"My model indicates we have the best chance of success if they come to us."

"But we could drive there in—"

"Correct. We could be there in thirty minutes. If that had been our plan, we wouldn't have diverted north on the county roads."

"A waste of time, in my opinion."

Gus nodded. He understood her line of reasoning. The problem was that she was wrong. "As we saw in Tyler and Ennis and Waco, driving modern vehicles—"

"Kick-ass vehicles," Sorrell interjected.

"Right. Driving modern, kick-ass vehicles through an apocalyptic landscape where people are riding bicycles or horses or even walking from one place to another... It doesn't always achieve the best results."

"You think we were attacked because we were driving vehicles?"

"I think the people left outside the government bunkers need to lash out. Who could blame them? They lived through this hell while we were safely protected from it. The first person who comes along in a better situation than they have... That person bears the brunt of their frustration."

Aimee shook her head in disbelief, then raised her hands

and let them drop. "Fine. You're the boss. So how long do we wait?"

"Another week. They will contact us within another week."

"You're sure of that?" Aimee pierced him with a stare.

"Yes. Because the model—"

She waved away his explanation. Sorrell made a harrumph sound. Neither was the type of person to trust in computers or technology. As Sorrell had reiterated time and again since they'd left Raven Rock, look at the situations the model had landed them in. It was true that very little had gone as the plan had suggested it would. Which wasn't a fault of the model. Gus understood that the program could only process information they fed into it, and they hadn't known, hadn't realized just how desperate things were outside the government bunkers.

"When this group from Alpine shows up..." Sorrell's eyes constantly shifted left and right, combing the horizon, on alert for trouble. "We just let them through?"

"They'll be expecting a patrol of some kind. Approach with caution, weapons visible but not drawn."

"Got it. Unless they shoot us. Then I'm allowed to shoot back. Right?"

It was as close as Sorrell came to a joke, so Gus smiled and nodded in the affirmative though he sincerely hoped no shooting would take place. Sorrell left to grab some grub before going out on patrol. Aimee remained, which was how Gus knew there was something else she was itching to say.

He sat back and studied her.

Aimee Taylor remained a mystery to him, even after all their weeks together. She followed orders without question, but she also spoke her mind when it was something he needed to know. In other words, she was a perfect second in command. What more could he ask for?

"Just say it."

"Long trip here."

"Longer than I expected."

"My men—"

"And women."

She nodded, though he thought he caught a slight roll of her eyes. When Aimee said *men*, she meant the people under her command. As in *mankind*. She probably hadn't been politically correct even before June 6th. She certainly wasn't going to bother with it now. "I'd like to start a rotation which allows for two personnel to rotate on pass for twenty-four hours. Since we're down to fourteen—excluding myself, Sorrell, and you—we can accommodate that each week."

"What does *on pass* mean, exactly?"

"They may leave base and are not required to perform any duties."

"And you think they need it?"

"We've been on the road since March 7th."

"Today is—"

"Twelfth of June."

"Right. It's a good idea," he admitted. "What I'm asking though... Are they showing signs of fatigue? Exhaustion?"

"They're fine. Our team is tight. They'll do whatever we ask of them, but time off has immeasurable benefits." She rarely stayed at these meetings long enough to sit, but now she did so in the chair across from him. Clasping her hands in front of her, she stared at them a moment, then raised her gaze to his. "No one can stay on point twenty-four seven. And sleep? Well, we all get what's required, but it isn't enough. It's taken us over three months to make a trip that would have taken less than three days before the Kessler Effect."

"All of you have performed admirably."

She waved the compliment away. "Twenty-four hours off

would help to reset their clock, their focus. It makes all that is required more ... palatable."

"Okay." He was wondering about the model. Had he accounted for fatigue? Burn-out? How would he adjust the program for that? "Make sure they don't travel more than a mile out."

She nodded, stood, and turned to go, but he called her back.

"What about you and Sorrell?"

"What about you?" She held his gaze.

That was another thing he'd learned about Aimee Taylor. She did not back down.

"Maybe after they make contact."

"Maybe so."

He'd actually thought it might happen sooner. He'd hoped that a few Alpine representatives would come walking into their camp forty-eight hours after they'd arrived. Galloping? How were people in the world at large traveling these days? He suspected they'd be riding horses. The question in his mind wasn't if or when or how they'd arrive. It was whether they'd trust him. And if they didn't, what would he do about it?

The plan hinged on trust and cooperation. And *the model* said... He smiled to himself at the way that Aimee and Sorrel cringed every time he used the word *model*. It said that the people of Alpine would trust them. He was still placing his money on that outcome.

He became aware of a slight breeze, closed his eyes, and enjoyed the feel of it. How often had he daydreamed about this very thing as he'd tossed on his bunk in Raven Rock? How often had he wondered if he'd even live to see the light of day? When he'd learned about the nukes in Chicago, he'd looked around and tried to imagine how the bunker, how any bunker, could survive a direct hit. He'd had nightmares about that very thing. Everyone in the KESLRFTF had.

Gus would take hot temps and fresh air over an air-conditioned underground bunker any day. Opening his eyes, he looked south, saw clouds building there, and wondered if the monsoon season was upon them. They had, of course, integrated weather maps within the program, but those were merely historical data. What happened on any given day could be drastically different.

And it was those things, the unpredictable things, that their fate often hinged on. He understood the limitations of computational programs. He'd never put his faith in quantum computers. Actually, he'd never seen one. Whether they would have been a help or a hindrance to humanity was as yet untested. As for AI, he suspected it had survived the fall of the lower orbital satellite array. He would have placed whatever money he had on the bet that what Artificial Intelligence existed had spent the last twelve months learning, adapting, thinking.

Computers weren't going away because society had slipped backward a hundred years. The things that had provided both hope and danger before June 6th, still did. But the pace of implementation for those things had been slowed.

Big brother couldn't watch your every move if you didn't carry a workable cell phone.

With the majority of people worldwide now disconnected from the grid, high tech could no longer use a person's social footprint to predict their next purchase or romantic interest or vote.

But the ability to do all of those things was still out there—waiting, watching, ready to jump into action once what was left of America reconnected. Waiting for what was left of the world to reconnect. If they stood a chance of surviving that shift, they would need the regional centers to be established and running. They would need the people to once again put their trust in their duly elected representatives. That, even according to the model, would be their biggest challenge.

So, he would wait.

Let the people of Alpine come to him.

CHAPTER 9

Dixie and Liam left before the sun broke the horizon. The day was pleasantly cool, though she knew that wouldn't last. The sky was a cloudless blue. A robin's-egg blue. The monsoon season for their area generally didn't begin until mid-June, and back in Alpine people were already preparing for it. Every possible container was positioned in the yard, ready to receive the water.

Water.

Who would have thought that water would be so critical? Though they lived in an area that was classified as semi-arid and they received less than twenty inches of precipitation per year, they still took for granted that water would flow when you turned the taps on. They'd brazenly taken it for granted, though they should have known better.

They should have been better prepared.

On the morning Dixie and Liam rode out of Alpine, the wind did seem to be changing, coming from a more southerly direction.

She studied the sky as it lightened.

No clouds at all, just a slight breeze.

"You look like a beagle over there."

She smiled because at least he wasn't answering in mono-syllables. The trip out of town seemed to have lightened his mood, as it had hers. "Excuse me?"

Liam tilted his head back and sniffed the air.

"Oh, that."

"Yeah, that. Am I missing something?"

"Wind's from the south. It wasn't yesterday, but it is today."

"So."

"Monsoon season."

Liam scratched the skin at the back of his neck, looked south, then shrugged. "Sky's clear."

"It can move in fast."

He squinted in the direction of the sun. "Seriously?"

"Where were you stationed before El Paso?"

"Lots of places, but mostly in the north and then overseas."

"Do you remember last year's rains?"

"I didn't get here until after that."

"Right. Okay. Well, normally we receive half of our annual rainfall between mid-June and September."

"Monsoon season."

"Exactly."

"I always thought a monsoon was... I don't know. Like a deluge of rain on a single day."

"It can be. Basically, it's when the Gulf moisture drifts west. Some years it doesn't happen, and that's when we have a noticeable increase in wildfires."

"Which is why you know so much about it—being Alpine's fire chief and all."

Dixie shrugged. "We need the rain, but I'd rather not have it while I'm traveling on horseback."

They rode in silence for a while. Dixie liked that about Liam. He didn't feel a need to chatter on. Maybe that's what made her an introvert—constant chattering over mundane topics exhausted her. This? This was a nice, peaceful ride through the desert.

Twenty minutes later they passed a family of javelinas that were rooting around on the side of the road. Looked to be a mom and five babies.

"Those are some lucky pigs," Liam said. "If I were on patrol today instead of taking this ride out of town with you, they'd be cooking in someone's firepit by nightfall."

"They're not pigs, and I think you know that. They're javelinas."

He brushed off her correction with a smile and a tilt of his head.

"A group of javelinas is called a squadron."

The deadpan look he gave her brought a smile to her face. "Just in case you wanted to know."

"I didn't."

"Okay."

"Don't have to know the scientific name of everything I put in my dinner pot."

"Did you not get enough to eat for breakfast?"

"I never get enough to eat."

"Long time until dinner. That's all I'm saying."

A smile cracked through his fictitious reserve, which was enough to raise Dixie's spirits. Twenty-five miles to Fort Davis. They'd move slowly, go easy on the horses, and stay alert. It was Liam's way, and she was comfortable with that. She was surprised to find that she was happy just to be riding away from Alpine. It had provided a sanctuary for her, for all of them. It was home. But even home was sweeter when you left it for a few days.

The land around them was barren.

A desert could be a surprisingly colorful place, especially after a rain, but those desert blooms faded as quickly as they arrived. All Dixie could see, in every direction, was brown—light brown, dark brown, dusty brown, even ash brown. All brown. No color at all except for the sky.

They had followed TX-118 north out of town, passed the airfield, the Texas Department of Public Safety offices, and an RV park. All deserted, or at least they seemed to be. Tanda had a pretty good idea of where everyone was at this point, and she shared that information with the Council. Most people had pulled in closer to town.

Dixie supposed in some places, like east Texas, nature might be reclaiming what man had built, but here in the desert that wasn't happening. Here, things would simply decay and then fall.

Whenever they came within sight of a homestead, Liam stopped and glassed the area.

"You came this way with Felicia?"

"No. We took the southern route, through Marfa."

She'd talked with Felicia about that trip. Felicia and Liam had stumbled upon a couple, even stopped and visited with them. Shared a meal. The woman had given Felicia a knitted scarf that she wore every day the temperatures didn't top eighty. Felicia claimed the scarf reminded her that good people still existed. Dixie didn't think she'd be receiving any scarves. She was beginning to doubt they'd even see another person. They passed a few deserted cars. Some had been pushed to the side of the road, others left sitting in the middle of the lanes.

Several road signs had been tagged with spray paint and a few sported bullet holes in a haphazard pattern. That could have happened before June 6th. If it had happened after, it was immediately after because people very quickly realized that ammunition was something to be saved and used judiciously.

What surprised her most was the lack of sound.

Even in Alpine you heard folks talking, people walking down the street, children playing, the clip-clop of horses. The road they were traveling on was more than just deserted. It had been forgotten.

"We didn't see downed power lines before." Liam walked his horse, an Appaloosa mare named Patches, around the thick insulated cables that lay along the road.

"Maybe the last storm we had—"

"Yeah. Maybe."

She was riding Sofia, one of the police mounts. Tanda had insisted that Dixie take the mare. "She's a good horse, won't tire, and she won't spook."

Dixie saw her first bodies—what was left of them—ten minutes later. A skeleton behind the wheel of a gray compact car. Another in the passenger seat. Bullet holes in the seat's upholstery visible through the rib cages. Images she'd rather not have in her mind. Liam caught her slowing and looking. He shrugged as if to say *such is life*.

They were approaching a gentle curve in the road and Dixie realized three things at once.

Both of their horses had ears pricked in alert.

Liam had pulled his weapon.

And they were suddenly, most certainly, not alone.

They rounded the corner slowly on the inside of the curve, hoping anyone with a gun coming toward them would be aiming toward the outside of the curve—the lane they would have been in if they'd been driving back when folks still followed the rules. They'd role-played this the night before. Liam and Keme insisted that habits die hard—anyone approaching would fall back on what they'd always done, which in this case meant driving on the right side of the road.

But, of course, no one was driving.

A man was pulling a wagon. He looked as if he'd taken a bit part in an old western movie—sun-baked skin, a build best described as sinewy, long hair pulled back in a band, no beard. He was wearing a battered cowboy hat, and his jeans and t-shirt looked as if a homeless person would have trashed them.

The woman with him wore cut-off jeans and a ragged shirt. If the man was thin, she had crossed over to gaunt. She looked as if she'd recently chopped at her brown hair with a pair of scissors.

Both the man and woman gave the impression that they'd been beaten by all that had occurred since June 6th. They looked as if they were simply waiting for the end to come. There was no energy about them. No sense of urgency. No curiosity as to who Dixie and Liam were.

But there was the wagon.

They'd made a sort of sunshade and fastened it on poles over the wagon—a large model red Radio Flyer with raised sides. As Dixie and Liam approached, two small children peeked out from a blanket that had been fastened across the front. A mixed-breed dog stuck its nose out between the children, sniffed twice, then retreated back into the shade.

The man and the woman pulled the wagon off the road and held up their hands to show they were unarmed.

Liam walked a slow circle around them while Dixie tried to engage the two in conversation.

"Hot day to be on the road," Dixie said.

The man simply nodded, his eyes pinned to the ground.

"Wouldn't mind some rain to cool things off," Liam added. He'd finished his circle, holstered his weapon, and nodded once to Dixie. All clear.

They both dismounted.

"We have extra water if you need some," Dixie said.

The woman made eye contact for the first time. Dixie had thought her to be older, but when she looked up it was obvious that she was maybe twenty. She licked her lips once, then nodded toward the children.

A girl and a boy.

The girl proudly held up three fingers to show her age. "I'm Abigail, and I'm three. Teddy is just two, but he can't show you yet."

The parents still hadn't spoken, so Dixie introduced herself and Liam.

The man finally said, "I'm Jesse. Jesse Bell. This is my family." His Adam's apple rose and fell as he spoke.

Dixie was reminded of the skeletons in the car. These people weren't far from that fate. They were almost... insubstantial, as if a wind might pick them up and blow them across the desert.

"And I'm Rose."

Rose. It was an old-fashioned name from a more innocent time. Dixie felt a surge of sadness at that, at the fact of these four trying to cross the desert.

"Headed for Alpine?" Liam asked.

"I suppose."

"You suppose?"

Jesse was even thinner up close—rail thin. Dixie had heard that description before, had read it in plenty of novels, but the man in front of her was exactly that. If he turned sideways, he'd be the width of a utility pole.

"Not sure where we're going, to tell the truth. Couldn't stay where we were any longer."

"Where was that?"

"Ranch house about twenty miles northwest of here."

"You've walked twenty miles?"

"Not all at once. We stop and rest in the hot part of the day. Walk some more until it's too dark to know we won't step on a rattler."

Dixie had poured water into a collapsible cup and offered it to the girl. She drank half, then offered the rest to her brother. When the dog whined, Dixie asked the little girl, "Does he have a bowl or something?"

Abigail nodded enthusiastically then turned and rummaged around in the back of the wagon. She turned back holding a disposable cereal bowl—the kind that would hold a single serving of Cheerios or Fruit Loops. Dixie filled it half full of water and the dog eagerly lapped it up, then licked her hand.

While she'd been tending to the kids, Liam had been pulling out supplies for the parents—a large bottle of water, jerky, a couple energy bars.

"How did you end up at the ranch house?" Dixie asked. What she wanted to know was if they had been there since June 6th.

"El Paso fell pretty quickly."

"We heard about that," Liam said. "A friend of ours, a doctor, was in the northern barrio."

"South side was even worse. Our plan was to make it to Rose's parents in Llano, but I-10 was impassable. We were forced off the road by the gridlock and eventually ran out of gas. The ranch house was just something we stumbled on."

"You stayed there alone?"

"Nah."

Dixie had refilled the cup and given it to Rose, who took a few small sips of the water, then passed it to her husband. He emptied the cup, drew the back of his hand across his mouth, stared at the moisture there. Then he offered the cup back to Dixie with a quiet, "Thank ya."

"There were a few families," Rose said. "At the ranch. Some good folks. Some not so good—lazy people who wouldn't have made it the first month if it weren't for everyone else pitching in."

"We did make it, though. Made it through the winter." Jesse stared out over the desert as if he'd find answers there, something that would help the last year make sense. "When we got low on supplies, a few people got mean. Real mean. There was a... a shootout."

"It was never the same after that."

"In the spring some left, determined they could walk to a better place. I told them that there ain't no better place. But then we got scared being out there alone. Couldn't stay on alert all the time. Couldn't protect my family if I had to sleep. Decided it would be best to move on. Try to find a group of survivors—a good group. Has to be some people left." At this he gave an imploring look to both Liam and Dixie.

Were they that?

Were they a good group?

Could they be trusted or was this show of benevolence merely another trap?

Liam pushed the supplies he'd retrieved from his saddle bags into the man's hands. Jesse stared down at the food and water as if he couldn't quite comprehend what he was holding.

"I wish we could give you more," Liam said. "We have a bit of a trip in front of us. We heard someone had set up camp in Fort Davis. Have you seen any sign of that?"

"Nah."

"I thought I heard a vehicle one afternoon." Rose pushed her cropped hair away from her face. "Decided I'd imagined it."

"How long ago was that?"

"Several days, I guess. Not really sure. Days all run together now."

The sun had risen and Dixie figured the temperature would reach the high nineties. She thought she saw clouds to the south, or it could be a mirage.

"My suggestion is you stay on this road," Liam said. "You're only about ten miles from Alpine."

"That where you're from?"

"Yes," Dixie said. "There's people there who will help you."

Rose glanced at Jesse, who nodded once.

"Like you said, like you've been doing, don't try to travel in the heat of the day." Liam could have stopped there, but he wasn't one to hold back.

Dixie already knew that about him.

"You both look about done in. There's a curve up ahead and beyond that on the west side is a small stand of mesquite trees. Rest there until the sun starts down. You can make it to Alpine by nightfall."

"And they'll let us in?" Everything in Jesse's tone screamed that he wanted to believe it, but the expression on his face said it would be tantamount to putting their faith in the tooth fairy.

"You'll probably encounter a patrol, half a mile outside of town. Tell them that you talked to us—Liam and Dixie. Tell them you're seeking sanctuary. If you're willing to work, Alpine can use you. We have doctors, a modest amount of supplies, and you'll have a place to stay."

"Okay." Jesse looked more confident now, looked as if he'd been given an answer that made sense. "I can work. Always been a hard worker."

Liam looked as if he wanted to clap Jesse on the back. One solid pat and the man would fall over, so he held out his hand instead. Both Jesse and Rose shook it. Abigail and Teddy had lost interest in the adult conversation and were playing with several ragged, stuffed animals.

Dixie stepped closer to Rose. "There are a few cars, past the curve. Past the mesquite trees. Take a wide path around them so the kids don't see—"

Rose nodded, then threw her arms around Dixie, and said, "Thank you."

Thank you.

For a little water, a pitiful amount of food, hope.

They rode on in silence, but twice Dixie looked back until the Bell family was no longer visible on the horizon.

TANDA HAD CALCULATED that the ride from Alpine north to Gutterson's Ranch should have taken three hours. But as Liam suggested, they didn't plan to approach from the south. Instead, they would angle west, circle around, approach from the north. Tanda found US-67 to be one of the most desolate roads in Texas. She'd be happy to divert off of it even if that change meant adding to their mileage. Crossing the desert, in her opinion, was actually a little better. A desert was naturally barren. A road, especially a state highway, was supposed to have some sort of activity. Instead, US-67 was desolate, possibly even forsaken. She'd never thought of the area where she'd grown up that way, but she did now. Some days she wondered if they were forsaken—left for dead, irredeemable, forgotten. Those thoughts plagued her on the tough days.

June wasn't the best time to view the Texas southwest. Partly that was owing to the lack of vegetation—scrub brush and cactus were the only things as far as the eye could see. Partly it was due to the lack of a human footprint, which she usually considered a plus. Not today. Not this.

This wasn't merely uncrowded.

It was uninhabited. The desert had been there long before her Hispanic or Kiowa ancestors had appeared on the scene. It would continue to be there long after the American citizenry had passed on. Neither thought brought her much comfort.

"What are you brooding about over there?" Keme gave her a knowing look.

"Why do you think I'm brooding?"

"You haven't spoken in two hours."

"Never have been a chatterbox."

"True, but you usually whistle."

"Whistle?"

"Or hum."

"Yeah. I guess I do."

They continued on, skirting around solar panels that had blown onto the roads. The Buckthorn Solar Farm was over twelve hundred acres and supplied power exclusively to the central Texas town of Georgetown. Tanda allowed Roxie to pick her way through the debris. "Nearly two million of these things."

"Solar panels?"

"Yup."

"In the state?"

"Nope."

"You're saying there's over two million of these in the solar field north of here."

"Yup."

"Huh."

She didn't have to spell it out to her brother. They needed to be thinking of a way to use these. It wouldn't be breaking the law to pick up the panels scattered across the road, or for that matter, to pick up the ones still in the field to the north. The place was abandoned. Everything in this direction was abandoned, and since Fort Stockton had burned they'd had no travelers approach from the north. One look at the former county seat of Pecos County, at the crumbling buildings and

empty streets, and anyone with a speck of sense would keep moving north or west or east. Any direction but south.

South was more desert, then Alpine, then even more desert, the Rio Grande River, and finally Mexico. Eighty-seven miles to the border crossing at Presidio. Or you could attempt to forge the Rio Grande at Lajitas or Big Bend National Park. Tanda had seen how wild and deep and dangerous the river had become in the spring when she'd traveled to Del Rio with Logan. She wouldn't want to cross it without a solid craft. And why bother?

Across the border there was only more of the same—desert, desolation, barrenness.

There was little wonder they didn't see travelers.

Maybe Keme was right. Maybe she was brooding.

When they stopped to stretch their legs and rest the horses, Keme nodded toward the south. "Rain's coming."

"Think we'll make it back before it hits?"

"Not a chance."

"Camping in the desert in the rain—hard to think of anything I'd rather be doing."

"Uh-huh." Keme drank from his canteen, then passed it to Tanda.

The water had a slightly metallic taste from being in the canteen, but it was clean and surprisingly cold. She was developing a real taste for rainwater. Good thing since nothing was coming out of the taps anytime soon.

"Tell me what's bothering you."

"Why?"

"Because I might be able to help." He wiggled his eyebrows. "I might know an answer you don't."

"Unlikely." She bent down and touched her toes, then went through a routine of neck rolls, shoulder rolls, and calf stretches.

"Are you done?"

"I was thinking of doing downward dog, but if you're ready to go—"

"Not until you tell me."

If there was one thing she knew about her brother, it was that he was more stubborn than she was. "Maybe I enjoy tossing around the worst, most unlikely scenarios in my mind."

Instead of answering, he motioned for her to continue.

"Two different groups arriving at the same time have to be connected."

"Okay."

"The fact that neither have made contact is worrisome."

"Agreed."

"Probably means they're planning an attack."

Keme looked to the left and right, then behind him. The Chihuahuan desert ran to the circle of mountains in the far distance—a completely unobstructed view. "We'd probably see them coming."

"Which they know."

"You think they're drawing us out."

"I do."

"You're expecting trouble."

"I am."

Keme shrugged, stood straight reaching to his full height, then bent forward and placed the palms of his hands on the ground—legs straight, form perfect. It was impressive given his height, or maybe he simply had longer arms.

"Now you're just showing off."

Straightening, he walked closer, reached out, pulled her to him, hugged her, and then kissed the top of her head.

She stepped back and shook her head, causing her long black braid to swing. "What's got into you?"

"Nothing."

"I'm not a dog. Or a kid." She ran a hand over the top of her head.

"And yet you're cuddly just like one."

Tanda swung up into her saddle and gave Roxy a nice pat. "Police chiefs are not cuddly."

And now he was grinning at her, but as they turned northwest, away from the single road they'd been following all morning and was visible for miles in the distance, he grew serious. "I agree that this development is worrisome. What we've been through in the last year..."

And now she knew he was thinking of Lucy.

Thinking of all they'd lost.

"It's made us twitchy."

"Twitchy?"

"We naturally expect the bleakest scenario."

"And we usually get it."

"Which is why this is only a fact-finding mission. We keep our distance, do some reconnaissance, return to Alpine, and present it to the Council. It's not our decision whether to intervene. The weight of Alpine is not on our shoulders, Tanda Kaliska."

She felt a literal ache in her stomach at the sound of her middle name. Only her *abuela* called her by her full name, and she was certain that Keme had done so for a reason—to invoke the memory and common sense of a woman who had been very dear to them both. A woman who more than once had reminded Tanda of her limitations.

You're trying to do everyone's job, and that is several jobs too many. You are but one woman. Don't forget that.

So much had changed since that conversation, not the least of which was the passing of their *abuela*, followed by the death of Lucy.

There was weight to be carried, that was indisputable.

Keme wasn't done lecturing her. "The weight of Alpine is on the shoulders of every man and woman in Alpine. We live and die together."

And then he cast a worried gaze to the south, where the thunderclouds were building.

They picked up their pace, made a wide circle around the ranch so as not to be seen, set up a day camp to the north in an outcropping of rock. Keme watered the horses and tied their leads to a mesquite tree. Tanda dropped behind the largest of the outcroppings that faced the ranch, inched around it and crawled forward on her stomach, raised her binoculars, and took in Gutterson's place.

The man had been a Vietnam veteran. He was tough and didn't abide fools. Tanda had shared more than a few conversations with him. He had preferred his solitude, even before the satellites fell. She'd once looked up his service record and read about what campaigns he'd been in during the Vietnam War, including the Tet Offensive in 1968. Who wouldn't prefer being alone after living through that hell? Who wouldn't seek the comfort of quiet solitude?

Matt Gutterson came to town once a month.

Bothered no one.

Picked up his supplies, had dinner at Penny's Diner, kept to himself.

The ranch, though—it was a bit of a surprise. The barn looked to be in great condition. The fencing was well maintained. The house was like most old farmhouses built in this part of the state—a combination of wood and brick with a porch that extended across the front and down both sides. From their vantage point to the northwest of the ranch, she could see three sides of the place.

Keme squirmed into position next to her.

He studied the scene in front of them for a minute, then two. Finally, he lowered the binoculars, nodded toward the horses, and they crept backward and behind one of the rock outcroppings before standing up.

"Vehicles look military," Tanda said, reaching for her water bottle. Her throat was suddenly painfully dry, and her heart rate had kicked up a notch. The old fight-or-flight mode was alive and well.

"Air Force. SKTVs—Search and Rescue Tactical Vehicles."

"Four of them?"

"At least. Might be more on the side we couldn't see."

"Do you think they're legit? Does this mean they're with the US military?"

"I didn't say that."

"Yeah." She leaned against the rock and studied the sky that was quickly becoming overcast. The smell of rain permeated the air. They could spend the night where they were, or approach and knock on the door. "No sign of Gutterson."

Keme shook his head.

"I'm trying to remember when I last saw him."

"Does he still come in on the 15th of the month?"

She snapped her fingers. "That's it. I did see him last month. We were having the outdoor dinner on the 15th. Don't know how he knew about it, but he came in for that. Even stayed and ate with everyone, which was unusual for him."

"So he should be back in two days then."

"Something tells me he's not going to show."

"What do you think happened?"

Tanda turned and leaned so that she could peer around the rock at the ranch. She tried to envision how it might have happened. "He would have been keeping watch, would have certainly been aware of their approach. With four vehicles—"

"Maybe more."

"That could easily mean sixteen personnel."

"Or it could mean four."

"There's something else," she said. "His sorrel mare isn't in the pasture."

"He wouldn't have left her."

"He sees them approach, knows he's outnumbered, and backs off. Takes the mare. Probably had a go-bag packed."

"But where did he go?" Keme glanced around, as if they might have overlooked both Matt Gutterson and his mare.

"The other scenario is that he stood his ground."

"Or he might have considered the US military to be friend instead of foe." He shook his head when the words were barely out of his mouth. "Doubtful. He wasn't the trusting sort."

"And if he stayed, where is his mare?"

"I have another question while we're throwing them up for examination. If the people who drove those vehicles are military, what are they doing at Gutterson's place? And why is no one walking a patrol?"

Their eyes met, and then Keme moved out to the left and Tanda moved right.

As they carefully, slowly, circled the perimeter of their position, the sky darkened and the wind began to pick up. But Tanda saw no other human being. There wasn't another soul for miles, unless they were in Gutterson's barn or house.

They met back at the horses.

Keme had been wearing a kind of sling he'd fashioned that held his bow and quiver full of arrows. He slipped it off and slid to the ground, his back resting against one of the large rocks. "We have an unexplained quasi-military presence, a missing rancher, and a storm bearing down on us." He absentmindedly reached for an arrow, checked its tip, replaced it in the quiver.

"Liam said to look for them to be well supplied—"

"The vehicles certainly qualify."

"Supplies would presumably include weapons, gear, food, and fuel." She'd seen nothing on the porch. No crates of food. No backpacks.

"Can't know about the first three, but they didn't push the tactical vehicles here. They must have had fuel."

"He also said to expect a large contingency of maybe a hundred people."

"This isn't that."

"Distinct chain of command, but even thugs answer to someone." She was thinking of Del Rio and Shaw and the battle that had resulted in Logan's injury. The gunshot that had very nearly killed him. "Finally, Liam said they'll have a specific mission."

"That would be the twenty thousand dollar question. But how do we get an answer?"

Tanda shrugged her shoulders and pushed her arms through her backpack.

"What are you doing?"

"I'm going to walk around to the northeast side. If I don't see anything concerning, then I'll proceed down to the ranch house, knock on the door, and ask."

"That wasn't our plan."

"Plans change."

"You really think this is the way to go?"

"I'm not waiting to let four SKTVs roll up on Alpine." She drew her weapon, checked it, and tossed him a smile. "Watch my back, okay?"

Keme nodded as he pulled out his rifle with a precision scope. This wasn't a time for bows and arrows.

CHAPTER 10

As Dixie and Liam approached Fort Davis, the sky grew darker and their mood more somber. They were now traveling through the southeastern foothills of the Davis Mountains. Dixie had been to Colorado several times in her life. She'd hiked through the Rocky Mountains there as well as the Sierra Nevada range in California. The Davis Mountains were different. Formed by volcanoes, the peaks and ridges were separated by flatter areas, so that it didn't form a traditional mountain range as much as it did a jumble of peaks and ridges. The highest peak, Mount Livermore, reached 8,383 feet and was home to the observatory.

At times they could see for miles. Other times, though, they were boxed in and could see only a few yards in front of them.

In the past that had never bothered her.

In that past, they hadn't expected trouble.

Except that now they did. They expected disaster and shooting and death. The last twelve months had taught them that those things happened on a regular basis. The last twelve months had taught her to be *on guard* in every sense of the word. Dixie could feel her adrenaline thrumming through her veins.

There had been close to a thousand people living in Fort Davis before June 6th. The area was considered a gateway to the Big Bend area for folks traveling from El Paso. It was also a big draw for tourists who came to see the national fort, McDonald Observatory, and night skies that allowed unparalleled views of the Milky Way. That was the past, though, and Dixie felt it with a sadness that was more profound than she had anticipated.

No one lived in Fort Davis now. The town had been decimated in the same attack that killed nearly everyone at the observatory. Only Felicia had survived, and she bore the burden of that every day.

Maybe Liam's thoughts were running along a similar track as his expression had turned into a scowl and his right hand rested at his side—ready to pull his weapon should the need arise.

It didn't.

Their mares made the only sounds aside from the wind.

They passed St. Joseph Cemetery, Mountain View Lodge, Mary Lou's Restaurant. The group that attacked the observatory and the town had set fire to everything as they attempted to retreat. Dixie didn't want to stare at the scorched buildings and charred bodies, but she seemed incapable of looking away. Liam reminded her to "stay sharp," his not-so-subtle way of telling her to pay attention, leave the grieving for another time.

Their road merged with Highway 17, which stretched south to Marfa and north to Balmorhea and I-10. The downtown district consisted of a few blocks, in the middle of which sat the Jeff Davis County Courthouse with its signature red and brick and stone. The glass was broken out of the windows, portions of the courthouse had suffered fire and smoke damage, and someone had taken the time to access the clock tower, destroy it, and spray paint a large black X over the clock face.

They rode past the courthouse, Hotel Limpia, a library, and the Fort Davis Drug Store. "Best ice cream around," she murmured. If Liam heard, he didn't answer. They were now less than a mile from the Fort Davis National Historic Site. Dixie saw no evidence that anyone had been through this way in a very long time. No sign of the military. No indication that they weren't absolutely, completely alone.

When they reached the US Post Office on the northeast side of town, Liam pulled on his mare's reins and Patches veered off the road and trotted toward the back of the building. Dixie was happy to slide out of the saddle. She hadn't realized how rigidly she'd been sitting until she stretched and heard her spine pop. When had that started to happen?

They tended to the horses, ate a protein bar, and drank from their water supply. The entire time, Dixie's gaze kept darting toward the darkening sky.

Finally, Liam motioned for her to come closer. He kept his voice low. "Weather can work to our benefit in a reconnaissance mission. The wind will help to mask the sound of our approach."

"And the pouring rain will keep them from seeing us."

She must have looked skeptical, because Liam smiled—a genuine, brotherly, we're-in-it-now type of smile.

"I never took you for an optimist, but yes—the rain, when it comes, will help to keep them from seeing us. It'll also keep us from being able to clearly see them. That's why I want to do this now."

"Okay. Do you have a plan?"

"We leave the horses here and approach on foot. Describe the layout to me."

"You've never been?"

"Sightseeing an old fort wasn't high on my list before June 6th."

"Right. Okay." She squatted in the dirt, which was thankfully still dry, and drew a rough map. "If we continue on this road, we'll come to the main entrance, which circles back."

She drew a skinny U shape. "You end up in a parking area that can hold maybe fifty cars. From there it's a short walk to the park headquarters and tourist shop."

"So we could walk." Liam moved to the corner of the building and looked almost due west. "We could walk across here and avoid the entrance?"

"There are a few trees that would provide cover between our position now and the parking area."

"They'll be watching that."

"Probably."

He stared out toward the fort another moment, then walked back to join her. "How is the fort itself laid out?"

"Visitor center here. Large parade ground between it and the quarters."

"Could a group be bedded down in those quarters?"

"There are more than twenty restored buildings, so I don't see why not—if the structures weren't burned to the ground like everything else in Fort Davis. The fort was originally created in 1854 to protect mail coaches and supply wagons." She added a few more lines to her dirt-drawn map then sat back on her heels. "The entire grounds are tucked into a sort of canyon and surrounded on three sides by sheer rock walls. It's a defensible stance, or it would have been in 1854."

"Probably still is today. The canyon walls would also protect the buildings from the elements."

"Winter weather, yes. Summer monsoons—not so much."

"How tall are the surrounding rocky outcrops?"

"Five to six hundred feet."

Liam glanced up, eyes dancing, eyebrows raised. "Glad you paid attention in history class."

"If you'd had Coach Redding, you would have paid attention too." She stared down at her map, trying to think what else he needed to know. "There are trails back here that lead to a scenic overlook. I suspect if this group is military, they'll have people up there."

"I suspect if this group were military, they would have already intercepted us."

"Valid." She tapped the map at the far western point of the fort. "There's a two-story, brick house here. It wasn't completely restored, but if there is a group at the fort, they could have people in it or at least an outlook stationed on the second-floor veranda."

Liam stood and walked over to his mare, pausing to run a hand down the horse's neck. Then he reached for his rifle and his pack. "I want to backtrack through town a little and approach from the southwest side. Do you want to stay with the horses or go with me?"

"Do you need me to stay with the horses?"

"Nah. They're not going anywhere. Just look at 'em."

Sofia and Patches both nodded their heads in agreement.

"Tuckered out." Liam pulled his weapon, checked and then holstered it. "We'll take a look, get a read of the land, and then come back here to spend the night."

"And if the storm hits?"

"We're going to get wet, but there is a loading bay on the other side. We can walk the horses in there."

"This building no longer has a roof."

"It has part of a roof, which is better than nothing."

"Indeed it is."

The walk only took twenty minutes, and Dixie was

surprised to find it felt good to stretch her legs. The malaise she'd experienced while riding through Fort Davis slipped away, and her anticipation of what they might find ahead put a bounce in her step. Who knew? Maybe the cavalry had arrived after all.

Liam stopped several times to glass the national park area. "I see four vehicles, but from this distance I can't tell you what kind."

"People?" Dixie hadn't bothered to pull out her binoculars. She would, once they found a better place to watch from.

"At least a few. Let's try and get a little closer."

When they'd made it as far as they could without attempting to climb the cliff face, they positioned their bodies behind a mott of scraggly oak trees. Dixie pulled out her binoculars, gazed through them, her heart rate accelerating as she did so.

"There's actually people down there."

"Indeed."

"Military?"

"They want to appear that way. Most are in uniform."

"Most?"

"Check out the guy walking from the porch to the barracks."

She panned left to right, saw movement, focused in. White male, medium height. Blue jeans. T-shirt. Was he wearing tennis shoes? "So not military."

"He's not, and watch…"

As they peered through their glasses, a woman in ACU trousers, a brown t-shirt, and combat boots walked up to the blue jeans guy.

"Now she *is* military—or was," Liam said. "I'd bet my pension on it."

"You're getting a pension?"

"She's done everything except salute the guy who is not military."

"Maybe his uniform is in the laundry."

"Possibly, but it's more than his clothes. He's not an officer. He's too casual for that."

"I count six, no make that eight, plus the two in the middle."

"Copy that." Liam lowered his binoculars. "I want a closer look at their vehicles. I'm going to scout to the south. Meet you back at the post office?"

"What am I supposed to do while you're scouting?"

Liam didn't have to answer that, because at that very moment, the clouds opened up and a deluge of rain began to fall. "Move the horses inside," he said, and then he was gone.

She jogged back, being careful to skirt around the same direction they'd come. The last thing they needed was for one of the Fort Davis people to spot her. If they weren't military, who were they? And what were they doing in Fort Davis, Texas?

Some instinct she hadn't possessed before June 6th told her to slow down and pull her weapon as she crept around to the back of the post office. She had the safety off and the weapon raised before the two people standing beside the horses even knew she was there and maybe that was due to the wind and the rain. As Liam had predicted, maybe it had given her an edge.

"Hands in the air," she said, moving toward them in the rain. "Step away from the horses or I will shoot."

As soon as Tanda made it around to the far side of the ranch, several of her questions were answered. She spied a corral and a simple, metal horse walker that looked like what her mother had hung laundry on. Some ranchers used it to keep their horses conditioned, but more used it to train horses. She suspected that was Gutterson's reason for having it.

This simplified version had a circular frame—one pole in the middle and adjustable arms extending out. Each arm could be attached to a lead rope. At least a dozen horses grazed inside a fenced area that had been out of sight from their previous position. She didn't remember Matt Gutterson having a dozen horses. In fact, she knew with certainty he only had the one sorrel mare.

Which wasn't among the horses she was watching.

Vehicles and horses. Why did they need both?

And where was Gutterson?

Several men moved in and out of the house. Though they were dressed in military fatigues, she wasn't buying it. The doubt that Liam had put in her mind was pushing its way into the front of her thoughts. These people didn't look military to her. More than likely they'd helped themselves to the horses as well as the four Air Force SKTVs.

Maybe from Goodfellow AFB in San Angelo.

Or Fort Bliss in El Paso.

She supposed it didn't matter.

As she watched, they set up a variety of bottles and cans on the porch railing, then paced ten feet away and proceeded to pluck at them with what must have been an air rifle. The sound was quieter than a regular rifle. Tanda could barely hear it, just a high-pitched, sharp pop. It had to be an air gun. Even these guys couldn't be stupid enough to use live ammunition on cans. They proceeded to drink from a jug they passed around as they cheered on the shooter.

On closer examination, she could see the damage they'd done to Gutterson's place. Windows had been busted out. A couch had been pulled out onto the porch. Apparently they had run out of cans to shoot at and were now using dishes from Gutterson's kitchen.

This was not the US government coming to offer assistance. This was a group of reprobates, trying not-so-hard to appear like the military, taking advantage of whatever or whomever they came across. And that was what decided it for Tanda. Sure, she and Keme could walk away. They could hope that whoever these guys were, they would turn north or east or any direction that wasn't south. But that only meant they would take advantage of someone else.

No.

As the rain began to fall, she made up her mind. They would stop this group here. She and Keme would do it. It wasn't a reckless thing to do, or maybe it was. Hell, getting up every morning was reckless. But the one thing she knew for certain was that it was a necessary thing to do.

Crouching behind a stand of Mesquite trees, she stuffed her binoculars back in with her gear, wound her arms through the straps of her pack, and attempted to stand. Her mind was still justifying the plan that was taking shape. Storming a house where you were vastly outnumbered. Attacking on their home turf. Going in even though ostensibly their mission had been merely to gather information.

The rain was now falling in sheets, completely obscuring her view, which didn't bother her as much as it should have. She was envisioning victory—fully and completely lost in her fantasy of retribution.

The blow to the back of her head—when it came—was a complete surprise. She fell forward onto the wet ground and wondered, briefly, if a tree branch had fallen on her. Then she heard the crack of a rifle shot, followed by the sharp whoosh of an arrow finding its mark.

Several in the attacking group were shouting and swearing and she heard one person scream, "I've been hit." Another sounded bewildered as he shouted, "I'm bleeding."

And then the pain in her head became too much. She attempted to pull up onto all fours, turned her head to the side to vomit and was kicked in the ribs. Tanda curled into a ball and waited for the next kick or bullet or knife. She waited for what seemed like hours but must have been mere seconds, and then she stopped fighting for consciousness and slipped into darkness.

She woke in the barn, her arms tied behind her back, her head aching, her ribs hurting, and two people with pistols sitting in front of her.

"Hey, boss? Sleeping beauty is awake." This was said by a middle-aged guy with tattoos down both arms, hair badly in need of a wash, and a missing front tooth.

"Good one, Dusty."

"Shut up, Delores. We're not supposed to use our real names."

Which caused them both to laugh. They had to be high, or stupid, or both. The woman looked malnourished, skeletal, dirty. She continued to giggle as the man picked up the jug Tanda had seen earlier, took a swig from it, and passed it to her.

The barn had been pretty well trashed—as much as a barn could be. Tools were dumped out on the floor. From where Tanda sat, she could see a few of the stalls. The doors had been ripped off the hinges and tossed aside. It was the blood stains on the far wall that concerned her the most. These two might be stupid, but that didn't mean they weren't a threat. And what had they hit her with? Who had fired the rifle shot? Her head ached, and she occasionally felt something dripping onto the back of her neck. How much time had passed? And where was Keme?

She didn't have long to think about any of those things, because a stocky man with a shaved head walked into the main area of the barn. He looked vaguely familiar, which she also took as a bad sign. He snagged a stool, dragged it across the floor, and placed it four feet in front of her. Was he actually worried she'd lunge at him? She was tied up and had a concussion and bruised ribs. She wasn't a threat to anyone—not now.

But she would be.

He must have read the fury in her eyes.

"Just like I remember," he said softly. "All that attitude."

When she said nothing, he leaned forward on the stool and glared at her. "Del Rio? We had a good thing going there until you showed up. I swore then I'd get even, and it looks like I've been handed a chance to do just that."

And then she did remember. "You were one of Shaw's guys."

"I'm my own guy." His eyes narrowed, and she thought he might hit her. He obviously wanted to. Instead, he sat back and crossed his arms. "Name's Peyton Steele, and I don't answer to anyone, *Police Chief Lopez.*"

He emphasized her name as if it were distasteful to him.

"But I was with Shaw, yeah. He was too stupid to get out while the getting was good."

"I remember now." She squeezed her eyes shut, then opened them again. Better. Now there was only one man sitting in front of her. Was double vision a side effect of a concussion? She couldn't remember. Probably memory loss was one too. "You ran into the desert, like a real coward."

"I saved my skin to fight another day. And looks like today is the day."

"Where's Gutterson?"

"I have no idea who that is." He followed her gaze around the barn. "Ahh. The old guy who used to own this place."

"He still owns this place."

"You know what they say about possession being nine-tenths of the law."

"An adage, not a legal fact."

"Well, I don't see anyone around here disputing our claim, so I'd say we're good. Consider us in possession—both figuratively and legally."

"Let me go now and maybe my men won't kill you."

Steele's grin sent a chill down her spine. "Do you mean your brother?"

Tanda froze. Even if Steele had caught Keme, which seemed improbable, he couldn't know that Keme was her brother. Could he? Who was this guy?

And then Steele turned and motioned to Dusty, jerking a thumb toward the barn door. "Bring him in."

When she saw her brother, Tanda had to hold back a groan. His hands were tied behind his back. He'd not only been captured but also beaten up. He'd lost his shirt, and the skin covering his ribs looked swollen, angry, bruised. But it was his face that made her want to weep. His left eye had swollen completely shut, and a cut had opened on his right cheek.

Looking at her brother, who met her gaze with his good eye, Tanda understood three things simultaneously. Their situation was even worse than she'd thought. Peyton Steele wanted more than retribution—he wanted to prove himself superior. And lastly but probably most importantly, they had walked into a trap.

CHAPTER 11

The two persons wearing Army greens did as Dixie asked. They even followed her directions to remove their pistols and slide them toward her. It would have been two against one, so she wondered about their quick compliance. It was almost like someone else had ordered them to stand down.

She picked up the pistols and stowed them in the band of her pants. Twice they tried to speak, but she silenced them with the raised firearm and a single word, "Wait."

Liam showed up twenty minutes later, dripping wet, and more than a little surprised to see how their situation had changed.

"I leave you alone for half an hour, and you go all Rambo on me."

"I didn't go Rambo. They're still standing."

"Sitting. Technically."

It was true. She'd instructed them to sit with their backs against the post office wall, pull off their shoes, and toss them to the side. It seemed like the easiest way to ensure they wouldn't attempt to flee.

Liam motioned for her to put her gun away and moved in front of the man and woman—arms crossed, posture straight, and an expression best described as no-nonsense.

"This rain isn't letting up and it'll be dark in another hour," he said. "When that happens, I suspect your compadres are going to come looking for you. At that point, I have to decide whether to start shooting. So, let's avoid all of that. Answer my questions—honestly and quickly—and we'll see if we can end on a brighter note than your bodies rotting behind this burned-out post office."

The two exchanged nervous looks, and Dixie realized that they weren't accustomed to the new order of things. They were surprised to find themselves in this situation. In fact, they appeared completely baffled and kept tossing looks to one another that seemed to say, *can you believe this?*

Where had they been for the last year?

How could they look surprised about anything? Because Dixie couldn't think of much that would surprise her. Not now. Not a year after June 6th.

Liam began with, "Name of your group."

The woman must have been of higher rank, if indeed they were military, because she took point on answering Liam's questions. "Region 8 Task Force, US Army."

"Name and rank."

"Jocelyn Garrett. Staff Sergeant."

"And you?"

"Gavin Montgomery. Corporal E-4. I'm a medic."

"What is a Region 8 Task Force?"

Garrett hesitated, no doubt wondering how much she should tell him. Dixie could practically see the woman considering and discarding possible answers.

Finally she settled for, "That would be best answered by the leader of our task force, Sir."

"And who is your leader?"

"Gustavo Martinez." She licked her lips, her gaze bouncing between Liam and Dixie.

Liam would look intimidating to anyone in normal circumstances, which this most certainly wasn't. Dixie kept a hand on her holster.

"You're both from Alpine?"

Liam cocked his head, then glanced over at Dixie. "They know where we're from."

"Seems odd."

"It isn't as if we have a distinctive accent."

"Maybe it's our clothes."

"Actually..." Staff Sergeant Garrett swallowed and glanced over at her shoes.

"Just say it, Garrett."

"Actually, if you are from Alpine, which you must be because there don't seem to be many people left in this desolate and forgotten part of the state..."

"Let's say we are, just for the fun of it."

"Then we've been waiting for you."

"Waiting?"

"And we were instructed not to be confrontational."

"Is that so?" Liam's expression brightened. "Gosh. Dixie, today is our lucky day. To think that we were worried about the possibility of a gunfight."

"They were petting the horses when I got here."

"Understandable since they arrived in those fancy vehicles."

"So what do you want to do?" Dixie was surprised to find she was enjoying this. It helped that they had the upper hand here, and Liam was in his element.

"Huh. Good question." He cocked his head toward Garrett and Montgomery, kept his eyes on them, but directed his question to Dixie. "Think they're telling the truth?"

"I do, actually."

Garrett looked relieved. "We wouldn't lie to you. Why would we do that? You're the reason we're here."

Which sort of stunned Dixie, and she could tell it surprised Liam as well.

"My partner and I need to have a private conference." Liam wagged a finger at them. "Don't try anything. She's a very quick draw with her pistol, and I—like you—trained in the US Army, so I'm a pretty good shot as well."

Both Montgomery and Garrett shook their heads, and Garrett said, "We're not going to try anything. We're just supposed to take you in to Martinez."

"Yup. Heard you the first time." Liam nodded toward a nearby trash dumpster.

The rain had let up, but there was more coming.

Dixie could feel it in her bones.

When they were twenty feet away, he lowered his voice and asked, "Do you believe them?"

"Can't think why they'd lie."

"Come on now. Both of us can think of a dozen reasons people would lie. Maybe they want our horses. They could slit our throats the minute we turn our backs. They could drug us and drag us away to some internment camp."

"Do you believe any of that?"

"Nah. I'm kidding. I think they are who they say they are."

"Still a lot of questions though."

"Exactly." Liam grinned as if she were his star pupil. "You're surprisingly good at this."

"This?"

"Life outside the sanctuary."

"Ah."

They walked back over to the medic and staff sergeant.

"We agree to your proposal. Sounds like it's time to meet your commander. Dixie, hand these two their shoes. Wouldn't want them walking down the fine streets of Fort Davis in their stocking feet."

As Garrett and Montgomery pulled on their shoes, Liam held out a hand for Dixie to pass over their weapons. He studied them a minute, shrugged, stuck one into the waistband of his pants, and handed the other back to Dixie. The two from Region 8 Task Force, whatever that was, exchanged nervous looks, but they didn't argue.

Liam walked closer to Dixie and lowered his voice. "The vehicles were G-wagens."

"I don't know what that is."

"Mercedes-Benz G-Class. Military variant. Expensive. They probably didn't steal them from a local base."

"Which means what?"

"They're not from here. Not from Texas."

"Raven Rock," Montgomery said.

"Excuse me?"

"We're from Raven Rock." At Dixie's puzzled expression, he added, "Blue Ridge Summit, Pennsylvania."

"Otherwise known as Site R." Liam untied Patches. "This gets better and better."

Which probably wouldn't have been how Dixie would have described it, but she would have readily admitted that her curiosity was piqued. These two were from Virginia? Had they driven the G-wagens the entire way?

And if so, why?

How?

Liam and Dixie walked their horses, who seemed oblivious to the rain. Garrett and Montgomery didn't attempt to make conversation, though both continually glanced at them as if they'd found an endangered species.

Thirty minutes later, the group of four walked onto the grounds of Fort Davis National Park. The historic buildings looked untouched by their current troubles. The military grounds had been in place for nearly two hundred years, and no one struggling through the current devastation had thought to retreat here. What gave Dixie pause was the stars and stripes hanging from the flag pole in the middle of the parade grounds. It didn't wave in the wind like you might see in a movie. Instead, it hung limply in the onslaught of the rain.

But it was the same flag.

The same stars and stripes.

To be sure, the US flag still hung in Alpine—at city hall, the local schools, Sul Ross, even Kokernot field. But seeing it outside of Alpine caused such a surge of emotion to swell in Dixie's chest that she had trouble swallowing. Tears stung her eyes and she stood there, in the pouring rain, staring at the symbol of a country that she wasn't sure existed any more.

Maybe it did.

Maybe this was the beginning of whatever was coming next.

Was this group actually from the US Government?

And was a man named Gustavo Martinez in charge?

She could hardly wait to meet this guy. They clomped up the porch steps and the man they'd seen earlier—the one in blue jeans and tennis shoes—walked out and shook their hands. He was accompanied by a big man with an intense gaze and a Black woman who looked to be in her mid-30s.

Gustavo introduced himself, adding, "Call me Gus." Then he introduced Ryan Sorrell and Aimee Taylor. Gus Martinez had warm brown eyes, and a firm—but not overly firm—

handshake. This guy had nothing to prove. Dixie thought he looked more like a college professor than a military man.

"We've been waiting for you," Gus said.

"So Garrett tells us."

"Would you like to change into dry clothes before we debrief?"

Liam looked at Dixie, who shrugged.

"Maybe," Liam said. "First tell us why you're here."

Dixie added, "And second tell us what you want."

Gus didn't seem surprised. Dixie had the strange sensation that not much surprised this guy.

He nodded as if he'd expected that response. "We're here because we're establishing one of twenty-four regional centers for the US government, and what we want is your help."

Gus expected to have to work harder at convincing the two from Alpine who he was. For a split second, he considered pulling out his identification card. Would that convince them?

It wasn't necessary.

The two exchanged a look, gave a slight nod, and it was done. He could tell by their demeanor. They believed he was who he said he was.

"We almost left," the man said. "Decided you all didn't look like the military."

"And now?"

"Those two are definitely the real thing." The man nodded at Sorrell and Taylor.

"Can we talk? We could go inside to my office. Get out of this rain."

"Let us see to the horses first—"

"We can take care of that."

"We'd rather do it ourselves." This from the woman.

Both looked as if they'd stepped out of a Cormac McCarthy novel. Lean and hungry. Skin tanned to the color of leather. Clothes that had definitely seen better days. Eyes that missed —nothing.

"Sure. Of course." Gus motioned for Sorrell to come forward.

"We don't have stables," the big man said. "But there is a fenced corral of sorts and a run-in shed. Apparently, both were part of the historical exhibit. I can show you where they are."

"That will work."

"Let's meet in my office in thirty minutes," Gus said. "We can't offer you a hot shower, but we've set up a place to at least clean off over in the officers' quarters building."

The big guy shrugged. The woman nodded. They turned to walk away, then pivoted back.

The man said, "I guess we don't need to keep your people's weapons. We took them out of an abundance of caution."

The weapons were returned.

When they'd walked off leading the horses, Aimee stepped forward. "What do you think?"

"Oh, I'm thinking a lot of things."

She waited, as they both watched the Alpine people lead their horses across the parade ground and into the corral. Finally, she turned to him and said, "Such as—"

"Surprise that they've survived the last year."

"Couldn't have been easy."

"Relief that they made contact."

"Same."

"Mostly though, I worry that they're going to refuse our offer."

"And what do we do then?"

It was one of Gus's worst-case scenarios and something

the program couldn't predict with any degree of certainty. "We honor that. Report back. Move on."

"Kendricks won't force it? He's risked his reputation on this plan—twenty-four regional centers for the new and improved government. His superiors could replace him if it doesn't bear fruit."

"Replace General Kendricks?" He shook his head.

"Not in the model, huh?"

"Nope."

"Guess we're good then."

"I guess we are."

Aimee left, and Gus waited on the porch where eventually he was joined by Sorrel. "Handed them off to Cavazos."

"You really think that's necessary?"

"I do, and I'd like to attend your little meeting."

Gus considered it, but he had a very small window to establish trust. Eagle-eyed, sharpshooter Ryan Sorrell didn't exactly put his own people at ease. Strangers tended to find him off-putting. And there was something else. Gus had the feeling that one or both of the Alpine people had been in the military. They would know what the presence of Sorrell meant.

"I'll meet with them alone."

"I'd rather you didn't."

"If we can't trust them, then this isn't the place for a regional center."

"If we can't trust them and they kill you in your meeting or kill all of us in our sleep, no one will know this isn't the place for a regional center."

"Are you always so suspicious?"

Instead of answering, Sorrel pinned him with an intense stare. A year ago, even two months ago, that look would have sent Gus backpedaling. Not now, though. Gus understood that it was Sorrel's job to protect them. Fortunately, Gus was in a position to tell him how to do it.

"From a distance. We'll remain in my office, and I'll keep them near the windows. You'll be able to see if they draw down on me."

"You're joking, but it could happen."

Gus glanced up at the darkening sky. "I'll have the lanterns on. You're a good shot. I trust you to protect me."

To which Sorrel merely nodded once and strode away, probably to take up a sniper position.

Twenty minutes later, the two from Alpine were back.

The man was tall, rugged, and probably Hispanic. His beard looked to have been recently trimmed and he wore his hair long and pulled back with a band.

"Liam Contreras," he said. "Formerly of the US Army until my unit disbanded and I was coerced into following some rogue commander for a few months."

"Dixie Peters." She, too, was thin, of average height, and had recently chopped her blonde hair. There was something about her eyes that hinted at what she'd been through the last year. Sorrow? Regret? "I was—I suppose I still am—the fire chief of Alpine. But enough about us..."

Gus shook hands with both of them, then motioned toward the sitting area that was in front of the window.

Dixie eyed the solar lanterns that had been placed behind the sitting area, giving the space a warm glow. Liam looked toward the windows, across the parade ground, then moved two of the chairs back a few feet so that they were out of the line of sight from anyone who might wish him harm.

Gus almost laughed. These two—they were pretty much what the model had predicted but better. Real life—four dimensional life—was always better than anything synthesized by a computer, even a computer running AI software. He moved his chair closer to theirs, which probably put him in the middle of Sorrell's scope. No doubt the man was cursing him. Still, no need to shout across the room.

"As I said earlier, my name is Gustavo Martinez," he began. "For the last twelve years, I've worked as a private contractor for the Army. My degree is in sociology, and mainly I formulated models for how society would react in any given situation."

"Such as—" Dixie was studying him closely. She was a remarkably good-looking woman despite her present circumstances, with a steady presence and focused energy.

"War, pandemic, terrorist attack. You get the general idea."

Liam ran his fingers through his beard. "Did you research any positive scenarios?"

"Let's see. Aliens. In some of those scenarios, non-human entities brought new and helpful technology to earth."

"You're kidding, right?"

"No, Dixie. I'm not. The US government wanted a plan on file for anything and everything."

"And did they?" she pushed. "Did they have a plan on file for the Kessler Effect?"

"So, you know what happened."

"We do." Liam's serious expression eased when he smiled. "Don't mistake us for a couple of hicks living in the wilds of West Texas."

"We did have a scenario for the Kessler Effect. I didn't realize that was what had happened until they confiscated our mobile devices and put us on a plane to Raven Rock. For me, the pieces fell together as we were in flight. Blip in the overseas markets, increased traffic on the Beltway at three in the morning, heightened security at the base..."

"You're thinking of something else," Dixie said.

He nodded. "I saw, or rather heard, a plane crash. I didn't

realize that's what it was at the time. And there was something else. The other consultants on the plane, on my team—we were all people without family to worry about. Not married. No kids. Later we discovered that we didn't even have living parents. They'd all passed from cancer or car wrecks or old age. We literally had no one that we would have been tempted to call. That made sense because the program had predicted a weak point there. If word of what was happening leaked before COG was established—"

"COG?" Dixie shook her head.

"Continuity of government," Liam explained.

"Then the chances of success dropped dramatically. They put us on a plane, shuttled us to Pennsylvania, moved everyone inside before they had a chance to question what was happening, and slammed shut the doors of the bunker."

"You were inside Site R." Liam leaned forward, elbows on his knees. "For how long?"

"Almost a year. We were underground for almost a year." Gus reached for one of the cups of water on the table and downed most of it.

"Long time."

"It was. I still feel a bit unsettled when I think about that year. Going underground wasn't something that I had signed up for. At least, I didn't think I had. By the time I fully understood what had happened, the doors were sealed, and it was too late to back out."

"How many people were inside the facility?" Liam asked.

"Several thousand."

"Soldiers?"

"Mostly, but also contractors like myself. And of course duly elected government officials—that was the original purpose of the bunkers ... to allow for a continuity of government."

"Is the president alive?" Liam asked.

"He is. Both he and the vice president. We temporarily lost the Secretary of Defense, but he was plucked from a vacation in the wilds of Montana and flown into the Mount Weather facility. The Secretary of State died from a heart attack the first week. Overall, though, the government is unchanged from what it was a year ago."

"So, they aren't all in the same bunker?"

"They are not."

Dixie crossed her arms, not fully buying something that he was telling her. "You can catch us up on current events later. What we need to know right now is, why are you here?"

"I was sequestered, for lack of a better word, with three other contractors." He told them about Ken, Paul, and Roslynn. Clarified what they each brought to the table. Explained about their assignment to estimate how much destruction was occurring outside the bunker. Described succinctly how they secretly began a project to create a New World Map, to decide who had survived and why and where.

"You picked Alpine?" Liam's smile had turned into a grin. "Alpine, Texas?"

"I didn't pick it. I simply helped to write a program that put in all available information including resources, location, and historical strength of the community. We each wrote a separate part of the program that then overlaid one on top of another so that the computer could analyze and predict." Gus shifted in his chair, sensing that they weren't buying it. This was the one thing they didn't believe? Out of all he had said, the creation of a computer program that picked Alpine, Texas as a thriving place for survivors was what they found incredulous?

He shook his head and tried again. "The computer identified twenty-four most likely locations, twenty-four places that the US government could support in an effort to reestablish strong communities. Alpine was one of those."

"I hate to hear where the other twenty-three teams went if you drew Alpine."

"My friends spread out across the map. Cody, Wyoming. Hood River, Oregon. Boulder, Colorado. And I didn't draw Alpine. I asked for it."

"Which again begs the question of why." Dixie had been watching him closely, listening intently, processing what he told them. "I'm from Alpine. Liam's there because he was forced south through a bizarre convergence of situations, but you chose it? Why would you do that?"

Gus blew out a breath and looked out the windows. Sorrel was out there somewhere, frustrated that he couldn't directly see the two people across from him. Aimee was updating the team on what was happening. If Montgomery and Garrett hadn't been assigned the first twenty-four-hour leave, they wouldn't have been wandering the streets of Fort Davis. They wouldn't have encountered Liam and Dixie.

And apparently Liam and Dixie had been scoping out the fort and come to the conclusion that they were not the US government. They'd said as much. They would have ridden back to Alpine, none the wiser. Gus would have waited a week, maybe a little longer, and then he would have had to accept that the program was wrong.

But the program wasn't wrong, and the two people sitting across from him proved it. That wasn't their question though. Liam and Dixie wanted to know his motivation. They wanted to know if they could trust him, not if they could put their trust in a few thousand lines of code.

"Maybe I chose Alpine because as a teen I liked to read and watch westerns. Maybe it goes back farther than that, to stories my dad and grandad told me. Or maybe it was spending twelve months locked in a bunker." He stared down at his hands, then up at Liam and Dixie. "When the program gave us the twenty-four sites, I knew which one I wanted."

"And traveling from Pennsylvania to West Texas... How did that go?" Liam watched and waited.

Somehow Gus knew that how he answered these questions, how he answered this question, would determine whether they would trust him or not.

"Not well," he answered honestly. "Barely made it out of Pennsylvania. Encountered resistance the entire way down."

"Resistance?" Liam glanced at Dixie. "What type of resistance?"

"Rogue groups with weapons. People who shot first and asked questions later. We came across a fair amount of survivor groups as well. We tried to assist those as we could. Montgomery being a medic helped. Memphis was bad. Hot Springs was even worse. We lost three of our team there. Had to skirt around the Dallas metroplex. We left Raven Rock on March 7th and turned southwest toward Alpine on May 26th. Before the events of June 6th that would have been a two-day trip. It took us almost three months."

"Why pass Alpine then?" Dixie asked. "Why come here to Fort Davis?"

"Some of my team questioned that, too, but the program predicted, and our experience bore out, that you would be more amenable to what we were offering if you approached us. I trusted the program."

"You act as if your computers were still working."

"They were. They are."

"How?"

It was a common misconception that Gus had come across again and again.

Liam explained it for him. "Every computer didn't cease

functioning on June 6th. What they lost was their ability to talk to each other."

"Exactly. That's how we had the data to create and run the program. It had all been stored on the servers in Raven Rock. All we had to do was direct the program how to put the information together."

Dixie pressed her fingertips against her forehead.

It was obvious she was struggling with something.

Gus exchanged glances with Liam who offered a small shrug.

Finally, she glanced up, eyes widened. "You chose Alpine—Region 8."

"Right."

"Your program told you it would be best to set up camp a short distance from us."

"The program as well as our experience on the journey south."

"You wanted us to come to you."

"Exactly."

"Then why did you leave part of your group north of Alpine?"

Liam sat back, blew out a breath, his gaze pinned to the corner of the ceiling. "Who's at Gutterson's Ranch?"

"Yeah."

"I don't know what you're talking about." Gus felt a tightening in his gut. "North of Alpine? Gutterson's Ranch?"

"Your group is here," Dixie confirmed.

"Yes."

"All of your group." Now Liam was on his feet.

"Yes."

Suddenly, the atmosphere had shifted, and they were all standing. Gus had the feeling that Liam and Dixie were about to bolt. That they would reclaim their horses and ride off into the storm.

"Explain it to me. Please."

And maybe it was that last word that caused Dixie to drop back into her chair. This time she was running her fingertips through her hair.

"It doesn't mean that they're in danger," Liam said.

"It sure as hell doesn't mean they're not."

Gus sat again and waited. There wasn't a lot else he could do. A minute ticked by, then two. It seemed like hours. When Dixie looked at Liam and he nodded, she pulled in a deep breath and addressed Gus.

"We knew about your group because of a billionaire named Isaac Thornfield."

"The tech guy who's trying to get the human race to Mars?"

"Same. Long story, but he came to Alpine to retrieve some of his people—"

"People who opted not to go with him," Liam added.

"Right. As Thornfield was leaving—climbing the stairs of his jet—he threw us a morsel. I suppose he thought it would unsettle us. He told us that the government had set up a base at Fort Davis."

"Okay. I don't know how he came by that information."

"Thornfield's appearance coincided with a group that arrived north of Alpine."

"Not us. Not the government or I'd know about it."

"Exactly. Which means that our people who went to Gutterson's Ranch are probably walking into a trap."

CHAPTER 12

Tanda stared at Keme. Had they broken his ribs? Was he having trouble breathing? He attempted to raise his head and look at her, but it only served to earn him a punch to the torso. She understood they were in trouble, but she also suspected Peyton Steele wanted something. They weren't dead. So, why was he keeping them alive?

"Tell me what you want."

Steele's grin revealed tobacco-stained teeth. "You're a quick one. Actually, there is something you could do to help me. We want Alpine's supplies."

"How much?"

"All of it."

"Not going to happen."

"Oh, really? You'd watch me kill your brother? Because I'll do it. I've no love for you and your kind, Tanda Lopez."

"My kind?" Her temper was rising, and she reminded herself that going ballistic at this moment, with Keme injured and her hands tied behind her back, would not be productive.

"Police." He said it with a heavy emphasis on the first sylla-ble. *PO-lease.* "You always think you're the smartest person in the room."

He paused, but she didn't have any response to that. In this particular case, other than Keme, she suspected it was true. Best not to verbalize that thought.

From the corner of her eye, she could see Keme once again raising his gaze to her. Steele's people were now focused more on the conversation than on him. She could feel her brother staring at her, but she ignored that and focused on the psychopath in front of her.

"Assuming I had the authority to do that, which I don't, why would I give you all of our supplies?"

"Because if you don't, we'll simply take it. This can go one of two ways. A massacre or a surrender."

"We will fight back."

He simply smiled.

"You doubt that?"

"I believe you'll try, but I also know that you're low on ammunition. We might take a few hits, but we'll win."

This idiot had no idea how lethal a bow and arrow could be. Or maybe he did. The two goons holding Keme each sported a wrapped arm. One from a rifle shot? The other from an arrow? Had she actually heard those things or only imag-ined them?

"Either way, we will take it all, take what is due us, and leave. But no one else has to get hurt, Chief Lopez. No one has to die, even though a part of me thinks allowing you to live would be letting you off the hook. We were doing just fine in Del Rio until you ruined it."

"Heard you the first time." Her mind was doing a dozen calculations at once. Of course, she wouldn't give him the town's supplies—not a single MRE. But he didn't have to know that. Get him out in the open. Get the numbers on their side. She could flip this situation then. She could defeat this man whom she should have chased down and taken care of in the spring.

"Half."

"Tanda—"

One of the men holding Keme up stepped forward and punched him in the stomach. Keme fell to his knees, but his eyes were still on Tanda. She shook her head. His eyes pleaded with her to put the people of Alpine over his life. But what good would that do? Steele wasn't an honorable man. He wouldn't keep his word. He'd thought this through. What he wanted was to leave Alpine empty-handed and defenseless, then he'd turn around and slaughter them. She understood there was no negotiating with people like Peyton Steele.

"Half," she repeated.

"Half isn't good enough," Peyton said.

"Even if I speak to the Council, even if I plead your case, they won't go for it."

"I guess we'll have to be more persuasive then. Go after the women and children first. We know about that little school of yours. We'll get into the SKTVs outside, speed through your pitiful perimeter guards, and hit the school." He shrugged. "They'll come around to my way of thinking—eventually."

She had to make this look real.

"You can't leave an entire town to starve," she reasoned. "Not in the middle of summer. We'd never make it until next spring."

"Not my problem."

Tanda dropped her head in mock despair. She attempted to speak, then cleared her throat. Allowed her mind to drift back to Lucy's lifeless body and let a tear slip from her eye. When she finally looked up, she put all the anger and resentment of the last twelve months into her glare. "Three quarters of what we have."

Steele stared at the ceiling, then grinned. "Three quarters."

"Fine. And you know why? Because the people of Alpine will pull together. They'll work harder than you've ever worked in your life, and they'll survive."

Steele yawned, crossed his arms, waited.

"If we do this—"

"No *if* about it."

"When we do this..." She allowed her voice to tremble. It wasn't that hard to do. Let people see what they want to see and hear what they wanted to hear. Let them believe that they'd won. "When we do this, you leave, and you never come back."

He shrugged. "Sure. That's what I said."

She thought Steele would drag them out and push them into one of the vehicles, but that didn't happen. Instead, he cocked his head toward one of the horse stalls—the only one with a door still intact. The two thugs who had brought Keme in dragged him toward it and tossed him inside. One went in with him, stayed for less than a minute, and came out laughing. "I'd like to see him get out of that."

Dusty walked over and jerked her to her feet. "Guess this day didn't turn out like you hoped."

He wobbled a little on his feet. How drunk was this guy? She could probably take him even trussed up as she was. Knock him down. Cut the ropes binding her. Run for the hills. That wasn't her plan, though.

They threw her in the stall with Keme, slammed the door shut, and hollered, "We'll be sitting out here. Guns are loaded, so don't get any ideas."

It was dark in the stall, but gradually her eyes grew accustomed to the absence of light and she was able to make out

Keme's form, slouched against one wall. She scooted over to him, wishing she could touch his face, offer him a drink of water, assure him she had a way out of this.

He struggled to sit up straighter and she did the same. Both of their backs were against the wall—literally, and there was nothing but darkness in front of them.

She waited an hour, then another.

She listened as several of Steele's men walked away.

The one stationed outside their stall door began snoring rather loudly.

"Tell me your plan," Keme said.

"We get them to Alpine and take them out."

"Tell me you have more than that."

There was a lightness in his voice that caused her heart to ache. He knew her so well, and she loved him so much. She hadn't always felt close to her brother, but that had changed in the last year. If there was something good that had come from this post-modern world, it was their dependence on one another. She couldn't imagine getting through this life without him.

"Did you shoot one of them?"

"I did."

"Hit the other with an arrow?"

"Yup."

"Good job, brother."

"Thanks."

"We won't give them our supplies," she added softly.

"Figured."

"But they can't know that."

"Okay."

That single word told Tanda that he trusted her.

"How did you get caught?" Keme asked.

"I let my rage blind me. I'd made my way to the other side

of his property, saw all their horses, saw what they were doing to Gutterson's house. I was so wrapped up in plotting revenge, I didn't hear their approach."

"Same."

"What were you distracted by?"

"You." He nudged her with his shoulder. "From your position, I thought you were going to start a gunfight while they messed around with the air rifles. And maybe the rain muffled their approach, but I suspect they were watching us from the moment we left the main road."

"Right."

Tanda became aware of the night sounds around them. The horses in the corral. The call of a night bird, and the yip of a coyote. She could tell by his breathing that Keme wasn't asleep yet.

"Why the horses?" she asked. "If they have SKTVs, why bother with horses?"

"I suspect they're low on fuel."

Which made sense. They'd stolen both. They had a backup in case fuel couldn't be found. And that told her something that she nearly overlooked, which could have been a deadly mistake. Peyton Steele was not stupid. He was overly confident, definitely on the dark side of things, and probably desperate.

And that last?

It could work in their favor.

Steele's men came for them when it was barely light. One man untied their hands while another held a shotgun on them. They were allowed to drink water from a rain bucket, splash it over their faces, take care of their toiletry. Then they were pushed—none too gently—to the side of the house adjacent to the corral and horses.

Steele sat atop a dapple gray, looking none too happy.

"Tried to ride your horse, Lopez. The beast nipped me." He shrugged. "If either of you, or your horses, try something stupid... I'll aim for the mares first."

Physically, Keme looked even worse by the light of day, but there was a glint in his eyes now. They'd spent hours whispering, going over plans and contingencies. The guard outside the door had slept through the entire thing.

They might have tried to run while darkness still cloaked the ranch.

But it wouldn't have saved Alpine.

Steele was determined to take what he believed was owed him. If her plan worked, they could stop this—without losing any of the supplies and hopefully with most of Alpine protected. Most. That was the part that turned her stomach. In a gunfight there was no way to keep everyone safe.

The ride back to Alpine went more quickly since they could take the main road the entire way. No need to circumvent the camp. Half the camp was going with them. The other half was back at Gutterson's, preparing for the upcoming bountiful harvest or sleeping off the hooch.

Tanda's hands were once again tied, as were Keme's. But this time they were tied in the front. It wasn't easy riding a horse that way, but it wasn't impossible.

Again, the thought of making a break for it pushed into her consciousness. Steele was obviously not comfortable in the saddle, and half of his men looked as if they might fall off at any moment. There was no doubt that she and Keme could outride them. But to what end? In order for her plan to work, Steele had to believe he was winning.

She spotted perimeter security before Steele did.

Keme saw them and halted his horse. She did the same.

Steele was riding in front with two other men. Dusty and Delores were riding next to Keme and Tanda—one on each side. Both looked hungover. Three other men rode behind. When Keme and Tanda stopped their mares, Steele's people shot past them, called out *whoa* and *stop* and pulled up on the reins so hard that their mounts tossed their heads and whinnied. But they stopped. Steele managed to turn his horse on the third attempt and walked back to them. By this point, the men riding patrol were close enough to identify.

Gonzo Watson and Quinton Cooper.

"I told you not to try anything stupid." Steele's voice held more than a warning. It held a promise. He would kill her. He would try.

"You want to keep riding?" Tanda chinned toward town. "Go on. They'll shoot you before you pass the Sul Ross campus. You want into town, you have to talk to the guys on perimeter patrol first."

Gonzo and Quinton had walked their horses closer, but not too close.

"Tanda?"

"What's going on?"

They were sitting straight in the saddle, one hand on the reins, one loose at their side so that they could draw the pistol or the rifle, whichever the situation called for. Keme and Logan had trained them well.

"We have a situation," Tanda said, forcing a confidence and calm into her voice that she most certainly didn't feel. "I need you to ride and get the Council, as many members as you can, and ride back here quick. These men won't move or threaten you, but we have to talk to the Council."

They'd taken in Keme's injuries and the fact that both Keme's and Tanda's hands were tied. They look saddened by what they were seeing, but not exactly shocked. Why was that? It was impossible for them to have known her and Keme's situation. What was going on here?

"I'll go," Gonzo said. Then without waiting for an answer, he made a sharp turn and galloped toward Alpine.

Quinton said nothing. Or maybe he said everything because his eyes were telling Tanda that he'd been expecting this, they'd been expecting this, and somehow, someway, they were ready.

Twenty minutes later, which was much too quick, a large group pulled up in front of Steele. Again, they kept their distance. Logan and Felicia. Had Felicia dreamed about what was happening? Had she warned them? The look Logan gave Tanda broke her heart all over again. He'd told her to be careful, and yet things had turned in one distracted moment. Akule and Dylan were there. A host of others. And then she made out Liam and Dixie riding on either side of a man she didn't know. Before she had time to puzzle that out, Gonzo and Emmanuel rode to the front.

Emmanuel studied Tanda and Keme, then he turned his gaze to Steele. "What's this about?"

"Name's Peyton Steele. This is my group." He motioned back toward his group of merry men and women.

To Tanda's eyes, in the bright light of a June summer day, Steele's people looked like a motley group. Well-armed, but untrained, lazy, delusional.

"What do you want?" Gonzo asked.

"You're giving us your supplies," Steele said. "Everything you have."

"No—" Tanda had to act shocked at the change in terms. She wasn't shocked. She understood fully what kind of man Peyton Steele was.

"Yeah." He glanced her way and smiled.

That smile made what little content she had in her stomach rise up, because she understood with complete certainty that she would have to kill this man. There was no other way it could end.

"Yeah. All of it." He turned his attention back to the Alpine group.

"Why would we do that?" Gonzo asked.

"Because if you don't, your police chief..." He again drew out the first syllable of police, as if it were a word of its own. *PO-lease*. "Your beloved Tanda and her brother Keme won't live to see the sun set. Then we'll come back, in our armored tanks, and we'll take what we want."

They didn't have armored tanks. They had tactical vehicles, which weren't quite the same thing. But she couldn't shout that. It was important that Gonzo and Emmanuel believe this man had the upper hand. They had to look shocked. Afraid.

They did look shocked, but they did not look afraid.

Miles slowly walked his horse forward so that he sat even with Gonzo and Emmanuel.

"Is this what you want us to do, Tanda?"

"Yes." She nodded her head. "Yes. We can't possibly *stand* up to this lunatic. He has the upper hand. It's the *last* thing I want to do, but it's the only way."

Miles stared at each of them, assessing the situation, and finally shifted his gaze to Steele. "Why are you doing this?"

"Because you people owe me. She owes me."

"I don't see how."

"You don't have to see. You just have to go and get those supplies. We'll wait here while you—"

"Hang on," Gonzo said. "You want everything?"

"Yes."

"If you want everything, it will take us days to move it all into one place."

Steele laughed uneasily.

It was a smart move on the Council's part. He'd be envisioning crates and crates of supplies. They were playing to his greed, and she knew it would help to unsettle his plans.

"You have until sunset. Eight o'clock tonight should work. Bring it to Main Street. We'll do this in the middle of downtown so everyone can see what pitiful leaders you are. And do not try me. My life was ruined because of this woman. She took everything we'd built in Del Rio." He stared at Logan as if he recognized him, then shrugged. "Wouldn't bother me at all to put a bullet through her head."

Miles nodded as if he understood, but something in Steele's voice had triggered Gonzo. Or maybe it was Steele's mare, uncomfortable under the man. She shifted. It might have looked like Steele was drawing on him.

Gonzo pulled his weapon and aimed it at Steele. But Gonzo Watson was an artist, not a fighter. His draw was too slow. Steele shot him twice, then turned and fired on Emmanuel, who had also reached for his weapon. Both men fell to the ground as their horses tried to shimmy away.

As one, every person in both groups drew their weapons—an assortment of pistols and rifles, shotguns and bows. The result would be a slaughter on both sides. Tanda's heart sank, her worst fears coming to life as she sat there with her hands tied to a saddle horn.

Logan was screaming for everyone to lower their weapons.

And Dusty Roberts, Steele's man who by all appearances seemed to be a washed-out reprobate, moved with the speed of a man much younger and pushed his horse next to Tanda. She felt the cold barrel of his gun pressed against the back of her neck.

"He'll kill her," Steele said. "I'd rather do it myself, but he'll do it if anyone else fires a shot. You got that, Dusty?"

"Got it, boss. My pleasure."

Tanda felt sweat drip down the side of her face.

Gonzo and Emmanuel hadn't moved.

Were they dead?

Miles was on the ground, checking them, shaking his head at one and then moving on to the other. Finally, he stood, his hands at his side, and said, "You killed them."

"Well, they pulled on me first," Steele reasoned. "The rules of the Wild West apply here. I was just defending myself."

Miles didn't argue, just continued to flick his gaze between Tanda and Keme.

"Hey, you must be a doctor, the way you jumped down so quick and all."

"I am."

"We could use a doctor back at our camp. Why don't you saddle up on that horse of yours and ride with us?"

"Why would I do that?"

Instead of answering, someone to Tanda's right pulled a pistol, cocked it, and placed it next to Keme's left ear.

Miles raised his hands in the air. "Okay. Fine." He reached for the reins of his mare and walked slowly toward Tanda.

She wanted him to go back. Wanted him to be in Alpine with the people of Alpine in case this went wrong. Hell, it had already gone wrong, and they'd barely begun.

"Eight o'clock," Steele said. "And don't even think about shooting us as we ride in or ride away. You might get one or two of us, but the others will make sure that Tanda and Keme die with us."

"You'll release them?" Logan asked. "We have your word on that?"

"Sure. Absolutely. Ride in, get the supplies, ride out, and we'll leave them on the north side of town. You can count on it."

Tanda knew what he meant was he'd leave their bodies on the north side of town. From the look Logan gave her, he knew it too.

Steele turned his horse, rode to the front of their group, and lead the way back to Gutterson's.

CHAPTER 13

If Dixie stopped to consider how quickly things had gone bad, she would have been frozen with indecision. She couldn't focus on that. Not now. Not when her best friend was being held captive.

Ron was addressing the Council—what was left of the Council. Himself, Logan, Harper, and Dixie. Four out of nine. It would have to be enough. They'd deal with the dead later. After they'd rescued those being held hostage.

Also attending to add perspective to the situation were Gustavo Martinez, Aimee Taylor, and Liam Contreras.

"*Last Stand* has been implemented," Ron said. "All children and elderly have been transported to outlying farms to the west, south, and east. Everyone who is left in town is able and willing to fight."

Dixie cleared her throat, glanced first to one side and then the other. Gus and Aimee sat to her right. Liam to her left. She trusted all three, trusted them with her life. How was that possible? She'd known Gus and Aimee less than twenty-four hours. But she'd seen their camp. Seen how their men and women respected them. Sorrell was here too. Sorrell would be an asset.

She did trust them with her life, but now she would also be trusting them with the lives of every person in Alpine. It was the right thing to do. It was the only thing to do.

"Aimee and Liam would like to speak to the operational aspect of what happens next," she said.

Aimee stood and walked to the map that was pinned to the wall. "They won't be expecting our vehicles, which we brought around from the south. Even if they were watching, from their position to the north they wouldn't have seen them. The G-wagens have held up in battle before. They're well armored, though not indestructible."

"And you have fuel?" Harper asked.

"Yes. Topped the Wagens off before we left Fort Davis, and brought extra as well. We have three vehicles which we will position here, here, and here."

West. South. East.

"We'll hold back until they have entered Alpine." Aimee nodded to Liam who joined her at the map.

"No way that Tanda, Keme, or Miles told them where our supplies are, and as the lead assailant said, they are after the supplies." Liam's expression was fierce, all business, battle-ready. "They'll enter from the north, but it's extremely unlikely they'll stop at Sul Ross. Their guy said to leave them in the middle of downtown, so we'll do just that. Plus, it makes sense from a tactical point that we would keep the bulk of it here—in the heart of your town where you can most easily protect it. They'll ride straight in."

He tapped the map, put his finger on the very center of Alpine. "The plan is that they won't encounter any resistance as they approach, and they'll proceed to the center of town."

"Once they've reached the center, we activate our pincer

movement," Aimee said. "It'll be like pulling on a drawstring. Alpine people close the northern route so they can't retreat. My people will come in from the west, south, and east."

"How many people do you have?" Gabe asked.

"Fourteen, including myself and Gus. We left three more back at Fort Davis."

Gus raised his hand as if he needed to identify himself. He didn't. Both Dixie and Liam had spoken to the Council in private the night before, explaining who Gus was. Explaining that he and his program were the reason the Region 8 Task Force had even come to Alpine.

"I'm not a soldier," Gus said. "Before this started I was a contracted analyst. My field is sociology. So listen to Aimee or Liam when it comes to military strategy. But listen to me when you want to know about people's motivation or possible reactions."

He had their attention now.

He had Dixie's attention.

How was it that she already felt she knew him so well? Could desperation draw two people together like that?

"Dixie shared with you the broad outline of the analytical computer program that I wrote along with friends of mine at Raven Rock."

"You actually spent a year underground?" Harper's eyes were wide, as if such a thing were difficult for her to accept.

"Nine months. Very nearly a year. If I had understood that going in, would I have gone? I don't know." He stared at his hands for the space of a few heartbeats, then cleared his throat and started again. "We are here because of that program. We're here because the data said that the people living in this town have what it takes to survive in a challenging world."

Gus stood, but instead of walking to the map, he went to

the window. The sun was slanting to the west already. They had only a few hours to prepare.

"This group that is approaching from the north, we predicted them as well. Not their names or how many there would be. Not exactly where or when they'd show up. But any good model would come up with the fact that the wicked sometimes survive—they're without moral conscience and they prey on the weak. There were a lot of weak people in the first days after the satellites fell."

"We're not weak." Ron's voice was a growl. "We're a lot of things, but weak isn't one of them."

"Exactly. But those people to the north are on the prowl looking for the weak, and now there are fewer of those people to take advantage of. The pickings have grown slim. It's why they're here, and you need to understand that you cannot negotiate with them. They want what is yours, and they mean to take it."

"And Tanda?" Logan spoke up for the first time since the meeting began. The words sounded like shards of glass exiting his throat.

"They'll kill her, as well as the two men with her." Gus didn't blink, didn't look away from Logan's piercing gaze. "They'll wait until they have what they came for, but once they're in town and in possession of your supplies, they will kill all three. Letting them go would look like a concession. It would look like mercy. If what you say about the three of them is true… If they're as solid as you say they are…"

"They've risked their lives for this town before," Harper said. "They won't hesitate to do it again."

"Then there's zero chance Steele will voluntarily set them free."

Logan ran his hands up and down his face. Sighing, he nodded, then motioned for Gus to continue.

"From listening to you all, I can surmise that Tanda and Keme and Miles think strategically and keep their heads in tough situations. She very intentionally conveyed the words *Last Stand*. She and Keme and Miles will know you've implemented it, and they'll expect the very response that we're planning. As long as they lie low and we move quickly and decisively, they could make it."

"Could?" Logan asked.

"Eighteen-percent chance." Gus looked apologetic. "With an error factor either way of two percent."

A stunned silence followed, and it was Logan who broke it. The last twenty-four hours had aged him. Could love do that to a person? Could desperation? Dixie thought it could, and she felt it, too. These people were her friends—her family. And still, looking at Logan, she knew that his depth of misery far exceeded hers.

"Tanda and Keme have been in worse situations," Logan said. "Miles has, too. Eighteen percent isn't zero. We proceed as Aimee has laid out. We protect Alpine, and we trust Tanda and Keme and Miles to do what they need to do in order to stay alive."

Aimee waited a moment, perhaps out of respect, then continued her briefing. "We picked up extra ammunition at our last supply cache. Some of it is the correct caliber for some of your weapons. My men are distributing it now."

"So the plan is for us to come in from the north and close the circle around the Gutterson group." Harper sat forward, elbows on her thighs, fingers steepled together, and stared at the map. "That means that we'll be firing toward each other. There's a chance some of our people might get caught in friendly fire. How will your men even know who is with Gutterson's group and who is with Alpine?"

"As we're distributing ammunition, we're also handing out red bandanas."

"You just happen to have boxes of red bandanas?" Dixie asked.

"The program predicted they might come in handy, so we made room for them." Gus shrugged as if no one should be surprised by what the program predicted. "My people have been instructed to hold their fire if they see any person wearing one."

"Something Peyton Steele's people can figure out pretty quickly," Logan argued. "Plus, Tanda, Keme and Miles won't have one."

"We've shared descriptions of all three. From what you've told me, they should be easy enough to spot. There's a box of extra bandanas by the door. Just be sure everyone on the Alpine side is wearing one of these. It'll help my people as well. Apparently Steele's group has stolen military supplies, vehicles, and uniforms. Because of that, my people will be wearing the bandanas, too—so you can tell the difference between us and them."

Logan was shaking his head. "They could kill one of our people, take the bandana, and wrap it around their own neck."

"It's going to happen fast," Liam reminded him. "From the moment they enter Alpine until this thing is over..."

He glanced at Aimee, who nodded ever so slightly.

"We predict the battle will be decided within an hour, maybe less. This isn't going to be something that continues on for days."

"I agree," Gus said. "I want to add that they'll be coming in cocky. They have three of your people—three people who are very important to your community. Plus, they just killed two. They won't be expecting resistance—not coordinated, significant resistance. That works in our favor."

The meeting broke up on that note.

Logan turned to go to the emergency triage center that had been set up on the west side of town. Dixie caught up with him as he walked out of the building.

"She's going to be okay."

"You don't know that."

Dixie didn't answer right away. She could see how much he was suffering. She understood a little of what he was going through. Hadn't she lost Hunter to this terrible tragedy that had covered the entire world? But Hunter's disappearance was something she'd had time to acknowledge and accept. The not knowing had been hard. Sure. But she didn't have to watch someone kill him. She didn't have to grapple with the knowledge that he was a few miles away, in the clutches of the enemy. That would have been even harder. So instead of answering Logan, she stood beside him as he sagged against the wall of the building.

"I woke up. When she was bringing me back from the Valley, and we'd stopped for the night. I woke up to her sitting beside me, weeping. I couldn't..." He brushed at the tears streaming from his eyes. "I couldn't speak. Couldn't reach out and tell her it would be okay. And I was probably only conscious for a few seconds. But it was enough. You know? It was enough to give me the strength to live. To have someone love you that much. To know that your death would break their heart..."

"Hey." Dixie waited until he looked directly at her. "Tanda knows those things. She knows that you need her— that we need her. She's got more fight in her than any person I've ever met. And Keme? Keme would move heaven and earth to protect his sister. At least he'd try to. As for Miles, his last gig was in Houston. He's tough. They're all tough, Logan."

"Eighteen-percent chance." He practically moaned the words.

"Gus is smart—maybe the smartest person I know, which is saying a lot since we have rocket scientists living in Alpine now. But he doesn't know Tanda or Keme or Miles. He doesn't know the reality of the last year because he spent it in a government bunker. An eighteen-percent chance might have been true before June 6th, but we're immeasurably tougher than we were then. Tougher and wiser."

Logan nodded, straightened his posture, and attempted a smile. "Thanks."

"For what?"

"The pep talk? Your confidence? Your clarity?"

"It's hard to see clearly when the people you love are in danger."

They embraced once, tightly, and then Logan turned and walked away. Dixie went back into Central Command—she always thought of it with capital letters—to gear up. She'd been a firefighter before June 6th. Now she was simply another defender of Alpine, and maybe for the first time, she was okay with that.

Gus had a dozen things to do before 8 p.m., but he looked up and saw Dixie Peters walking toward the Sul Ross Campus, and he paused. She noticed him and offered a small wave. When she reached his side, they turned and looked out over Alpine.

"Are you surveying the battlefield?" she asked.

"Nah. Just wanted to steal a few quiet moments."

"Right. I'll just—" She waved toward the building where the details of the night's defensive strategy were being hammered out.

Gus knew they were all feeling antsy, but they were as prepared as they could be. So he said, "Actually, if you have a minute, can we talk?"

"Of course, but do you mind if we move while we do so? I'm feeling... antsy."

He nodded and they began to walk a circuit around the Sul Ross campus, which was built on a hill that overlooked the town of Alpine. They walked past the Morelock Academic Building, a computer resource building, Lawrence Hall. Each building had signage proclaiming its name and purpose. Landscaping consisted of various types of cacti, which had managed to thrive in spite of the last year. They passed Ferguson Hall. Fletcher Hall. When Dixie paused to stare out over I-90, he nodded toward the shade of the building and they sat, their backs against it, their eyes on the scene of their fate.

"Had you ever been to Alpine?"

"No." He laughed. "I'd never been to Texas."

"Must look strange to you."

"Both this town and this campus look surreal, if I were honest. As if it were carved out of the surrounding desert. As if it were a movie set."

"And yet it's our home."

"I know it is."

"This university opened in 1920. Seventy-seven students enrolled."

"Who was Sul Ross?"

She turned toward him and smiled. "Confederate States Army general, 19th governor of Texas, and 4th president of the Agricultural and Mechanical College of Texas, now called Texas A&M."

"Wow. Did they make you learn that in school?"

"Are you kidding me? You have to learn it to be a resident of Alpine."

"I should start taking notes then." Gus thought it felt good to banter back and forth. How long had it been since he'd simply had a conversation with someone? Of course, this conversation tiptoed around the fact that Dixie's town was about to be attacked and three of her best friends were being held hostage. The thought sobered him.

"Sul Ross University serves the entire Big Bend region and has... *had* campuses in Del Rio, Uvalde, Eagle Pass, even Castroville. It's a fine school, but more than that it's an important part of the history of Alpine."

He didn't interrupt. Gus thought he needed to understand this place, this woman, these people—before the first shots were fired.

"When you live in a town of six thousand, everyone knows everyone else," Dixie continued. "The local schools become something you rally around. They represent you, and you support them. I guess what I'm saying is that this campus is more than just a collection of buildings on a hill. This institution *is* Alpine—or what's left of it."

That sat between them a while. The day was hot—of course it was. West Texas in June was supposed to include blistering heat. The rains of the day before had stopped, the sky was cloudless, and the air was clean. Gus let the silence wash over him. He became aware of the birds hopping along the path, the breeze in the trees, the sight of people scurrying around below.

"This isn't your first battle," he said.

"No. It's not."

"Are you worried that Steele will—"

"Prevail? No. He won't. But there will be a cost. There is always a cost. Gonzo. Emmanuel." She shook her head. "They woke up this morning not understanding that it would be their last day to walk this Earth."

"But that was also true before June 6th. People woke, drank their coffee, went to work not knowing they were going to die in a car wreck or a plane crash or a terrorist attack."

"Wow."

"Wow?"

"If this is your idea of a pep talk, you need to work on it."

"Was I supposed to be giving you a pep talk?" He was relieved when Dixie smiled and shook her head in mock despair. He thought it was mock.

"How's this?" The sun was now high in the sky, and the day was growing warm. The shade felt nice. It felt like a reprieve from what they were about to experience. "You people—Alpine's people—are nothing like what I envisioned."

Dixie put her right hand over her heart. "Your program let you down?"

He laughed. She wasn't the first person to tease him about *his program*. "It didn't let me down, but a program can only deliver statistics, data, probability, and calculations. When you and Liam walked into Fort Davis, having disarmed two of my people, it's like—"

"Do not say it's like we walked out of a movie."

"Nah, though it was that, too. But it was more like the thing I had been so sure of, the thing that I had insisted still existed, did. You two proved that."

"And what was this thing?" Dixie didn't shy away from his gaze.

She stared at him and waited, causing him to feel a bit tongue-tied. Her eyes were the loveliest blue he'd seen— reminding him of summer skies and cool water.

"Good people," He cleared his throat. "Folks who are tough,

loyal, and will do what it takes to survive. People who chose the right side of things."

"Don't make us out to be saints. Liam has a terrible habit of forgetting he's no longer in the military. Or maybe he is. I'm not sure how that works. Tanda has a fierce temper, which she keeps in check most of the time. And Keme is one of the most stubborn people I've ever had the pleasure of knowing."

"What about you?"

"Me?"

"Yes, Dixie Peters. What is not so perfect about you?"

He'd meant it as a joke, but he could tell she took the question seriously.

Her gaze had returned to the main road leading into town. "I hold on too fiercely to the past. Tend to expect the worst. Forget to stop and enjoy life—what's left of it."

"Those aren't terrible things."

Instead of agreeing or disagreeing with him, she turned the tables. "What about you? What are your faults?"

"I didn't call them faults."

"Okay, what is not so perfect about you, Gustavo Martinez?"

Yikes. He supposed he'd asked for this. But it didn't feel as intrusive as he thought it might. It felt as if he were throwing off the cloak that had been wrapped around him for the last year and stepping into the stream of life.

So, he told her how he had a habit of being an introvert, even around people he considered to be friends. How he liked, even preferred, the predictability of academic studies and statistical charts and computer programming. He confessed to her how much he regretted the years he'd spent not actually participating in life in a meaningful way.

By the time they stood and walked back into the administration building, Gus felt something he hadn't in a very long time. Of course, he'd grown close to Aimee and Sorrell and all of his team. He'd even counted Ken and Paul and Roslynn as his friends. But he understood that what was happening here, on this day, went deeper than that. He was making a commitment unlike any promise he'd ever given. One that even outweighed the decision to travel from Pennsylvania to West Texas in search of a group of rugged survivors. He was putting his life and the lives of his people on the line for the town of Alpine. For the people of Alpine.

He cared about what happened to them.

He was confident they would prevail.

And he understood, as Dixie had said, that there would be a cost.

CHAPTER 14

Steele's anger grew as they rode back to the Gutterson
ranch. By the time they reached it, raw fury emanated
from the man. They'd barely arrived when he yanked
Tanda from her saddle and literally dragged her to an area
beside the corral.

His men quickly caught on to the fact that something was
happening. They gathered on the corral side of the area,
leaning over the fence, and they forced Keme and Miles to the
front of the group. No doubt, Steele wanted both of them to
have a front-row seat. Even the people in Gutterson's house
came out to see the entertainment. They watched and pointed
and murmured as Steele fumbled with the rope around
Tanda's wrists, untied it, then forced her arms around the
center post of a horse walker and cuffed her there.

Cuffed her with her own handcuffs that she had so
thoughtfully been carrying with her gear the day before.

"What are you doing, Steele?"

"What am I doing?" His voice rose to a shout. "What am I
doing? How dare you signal your people to draw on me?"

"I didn't—"

"Shut up!" He stormed away.

Maybe he meant to leave her there. Give her a few hours in the sun to teach her a lesson. But the man was becoming completely unhinged, so Tanda suspected it was something worse than that. When he returned carrying a cage covered with a tarp, her heart sank. She could hear the rattle from inside.

"Dusty," he barked.

The man didn't look particularly eager to answer his boss, but he walked closer, eyeing the cage the entire time.

"Take off her shoes. And her socks."

Tanda tried to squirm away from him, but Steele drew his gun, cocked it, and pointed it at her. "This'll be faster," he murmured. "Your choice."

She froze, then allowed Dusty to remove her shoes and socks.

"Now roll up her pants."

The man actually giggled as he did so. She wanted to kick him in the mouth. But she didn't because she could survive a rattlesnake bite. She wouldn't survive a bullet fired from three feet away.

"When I give you the word, you open the door on that cage."

"But—"

"Just do it, Dusty. Or you'll be the third man I shoot today."

Before Steele left, he knelt down in front of her. "I'm going to enjoy watching this."

"You're getting what you want. You don't have to kill me now."

"Nope. I don't have to." His anger had abated somewhat, and his eyes now seemed to dance with amusement. "But I want to. And who knows? Maybe you'll get lucky and live long enough for me to put a bullet in your head tonight."

Tanda was aware of Miles and Keme shouting at Steele, begging him to "stop this madness." He wasn't going to stop. Peyton Steele was in his element. He'd unleashed his inner beast, and that beast had set its gaze pinned on Tanda.

Instead of begging for her life, she closed her eyes and envisioned her grandmother. Her *abuela* was the calmest, wisest person she'd ever known. Tanda pictured her face and used that image to slow her heart rate. Hadn't she read that a rapid heart rate accelerated the effects of rattlesnake venom? She opened her eyes and saw Dusty move toward the crate. Twice, he leaned forward to unfasten the latch and twice he jerked back. Steele's men at the fence hooted and catcalled. Beneath the commotion, she could hear Keme and Miles calling to her.

But her attention was on the now opened cage.

The rattler didn't come out immediately.

Why would it? The cage was cool. But snakes like to crawl and perhaps this one understood that it had been granted freedom. It slithered out into the sun. Its tongue darted back and forth, testing the air, sensing the possibilities.

Tanda's heart was racing, in spite of her attempt to stay calm. Sweat poured off her as she tried to remember what she'd learned in the first aid class she'd taken. Snakes detected humans through vibration, an oddly developed sense of taste and smell in the roof of their mouth. They also possessed the ability to detect infrared radiation. She couldn't do anything about her body heat or her smell, but she could remain perfectly still.

As everything in her fight-or-flight brain screamed for her to run, she forced her body into complete stillness.

The snake showed no signs of being disturbed by the noise

from the onlookers. But there was no doubt it was aware of her. She was sitting on the ground, handcuffed to the metal pole. She scooted slowly, attempting to put the pole between her and the reptile. It was a big one. She'd never liked snakes. She'd shot a few when people called into the police station because one was sunning up against their house. She wouldn't be shooting this one.

The snake began to coil into its ominous S-shape. Its body flattened out. Its head raised ever so slightly.

The crowd at the corral fence—including Keme and Miles—had grown silent.

The unmistakable sound of the snake's rattle filled the air, reminding her of a maraca. Reminding her of pain and death and the shortness of life.

Tanda was close enough to see the muscles in its neck tense. She would later swear that it fixed its eyes on her. And then it struck so quickly that she wasn't certain it had happened. Pain sliced through her ankle as if someone had thrust a piece of glass into the joint. She was too petrified to scream, watching and aware that it was about to strike again.

And then she heard the crack of a rifle.

The snake fell into the dust, flopped once.

And suddenly everyone was shouting. She heard someone say, "Came from the north."

Another person hollered, "No, I think it was the west. Behind us."

She looked over at Keme and Miles. Keme was attempting to throw off three of Steele's men. Miles was trying to reason with Steele. "Just let me look at her."

"Later. Go inside and see to my people first."

Then Steele strode away, determined to find and kill the person who had fired that rifle. Someone was out there. A guardian angel? Or Matt Gutterson? As the pain spread up her leg, she closed her eyes, focused again on her *abuela* and the life she'd had before, pushed away the thought of the pain and the venom. She took deep breaths in, long breaths out as she heard Steele send his men out to scout the area.

By the time someone thought to drag her back into the horse stall, she was aware of a burning sensation as well as a throbbing in her ankle. She'd been stung by a scorpion several times—a pretty common occurrence when you lived in West Texas. That terrible pain wasn't even close to what she was enduring now. The world seemed to spin, and she wondered if this was it. Was she dying? Had she survived the last twelve months to die at the hands of a man like Peyton Steele?

She turned her head and vomited.

They'd removed the cuffs and retied her hands—again in the front. She lay on the dirt floor, sweating, her body shaking, bolts of pain pulsing through her ankle, wondering if there was something else she could or should do.

Tourniquets had been proven ineffective, even detrimental.

No way she could suck the venom out of her own ankle— the bite had been on the outside. Plus, that had also been debunked.

She forced her mind to move away from the pain and remember the first aid class. Stay calm, remove tight clothing, clean the area. She was still without socks and shoes. She had nothing to clean the area, so all she could do was focus on her breathing, lower her heart rate, wait for her adrenaline levels to drop.

Eventually Keme, then Miles, were thrown into the stall with her. One of Peyton's people had taken their shoes as well —a pretty effective way to make sure they didn't run out into the desert. Another had tied their hands together. Whether they'd intentionally tied them in the front or were simply distracted was hard to say, but it at least allowed the two men to attempt to care for Tanda.

"You're not dead," Miles joked. "First positive turn of the day."

Keme settled beside her, then clasped her hand while Miles examined the bite.

"Tanda versus the rattler," Keme said. "This will become a story your children tell to their children."

"I don't have any children," she said.

"Give it time."

"Not exactly a dry bite given the swelling, but..." Miles' face came into view, hovering over her. "Look at me, Tanda. Follow my finger. Okay, now focus here." He held up his finger to the right side of his head, still studying her pupils.

"Are you nauseous?"

"I threw up."

"Tingling?"

"At first. Now I can't really feel anything."

"I'd rather clean the bite, but until I can..."

"Am I dying?"

"Nope."

"You're sure? You're not just saying that?" She wanted it to sound funny, but tears stung her eyes and her throat felt as if it were closing.

"I'm sure. You have two puncture wounds, but based on the fact that the swelling is localized, your breathing is good, your pupils equally responsive... I think we got lucky here." He took off his shirt, tore it into strips, and tied the strips together, carefully wrapping her ankle.

She wanted to laugh.

Instead, she began to cry.

Keme patted her shoulder. Miles grinned and sat beside

her. The two helped her to a sitting position, though they insisted she lean against the wall of the horse stall.

"You still need to rest," Miles cautioned. "But it's better to have your heart elevated above the bite location."

"Who did Peyton want you to look at?" Keme asked Miles.

"Well, there were the two people you apparently shot. One with a bow, one with a rifle?"

"Yup."

"Cleaned those wounds as best I could. Two more of his people have been down for the better part of a week. One has a pretty nasty infection in a wound on her leg. Without antibi-otics—" He blew out a breath and rubbed at his right eye. "The other has a raging tooth infection. I suggested he gargle with saltwater, but again, without antibiotics..."

His words drifted away.

It had been an exhausting day, and it wasn't yet noon.

Tanda forced her thoughts away from the snake bite and back toward their current situation. "Who was riding with Dixie and Liam?"

Miles told them about the Region 8 Task Force, about Gustavo Martinez's computer program that had picked twenty-four regional centers.

"And Alpine was one?" Tanda felt as if this were all some bizarre dream. Was she really in a horse stall with a rattlesnake bite and two of the people most dear to her sitting at her side? Was the US government actually coming to Alpine?

"It makes sense," Keme said. "We're a good distance from a major urban area. We have natural resources. We've survived."

"Pretty much the way Gus explained it." Miles let out a big breath. "Liam and Dixie figured out that if the government was at Fort Davis, they weren't here—at Gutterson's. They thought you might be walking into a trap. By the way, where is Gutterson?"

"We haven't seen him, and apparently neither has Steele. I suppose he's the person who saved me. Must have been hiding back in the hills, doing reconnaissance of this place from a distance. The shot he made was pretty incredible. If the snake had struck again—" Tanda didn't want to let her thoughts go there. "Remind me to thank him."

"You said he was a Vietnam vet," Keme reminded her. "My guess is the man's still good with a rifle and a scope."

"So he's watching, biding his time. That could work to our advantage." She supposed she must be feeling better. Her emotions had been entirely occupied by her near-death experience, but now she was thinking about Gonzo and Emmanuel. They were two good men, and they had not deserved to die the way they had. The emotions she'd kept in check to lower her heart rate came rushing back. When Peyton had shot Gonzo and Emmanuel, she'd wanted to claw his eyes out—or better yet, put her hands around his neck and squeeze until the last breath of life escaped his lying lips.

"Take it easy, Tanda." Miles reached for her hand and held it. "I want you to keep your heart rate slow."

She nodded. He was right. Miles Turner was usually right.

"Remember the first time I came to your ranch?"

"I do."

"You and Zeus living on Old Ranch Road."

"That dog saved my life. When I wasn't sure I wanted to keep going, he'd scratch on the door to go outside, then insist I walk with him."

"A faithful companion, that one." Keme squeezed Tanda's other hand. "Maybe we need to get you a dog."

"I still go up there once a month," Miles said. "Just to check on things."

"That day we came up, you told me you weren't practicing medicine anymore."

"I did."

"Glad you changed your mind."

"Me too, my friend. Me too."

Tanda knew she needed to sleep, but her thoughts kept careening from one facet of their situation to another. Finally, she returned to the subject of the Region 8 people. "Tell me more about Gustavo Martinez."

So Miles did—how he wasn't exactly military, how he and his friends had developed a model to predict survivors, how he'd chosen Alpine.

"The government still exists?" Keme peered at Miles with his one good eye.

"Apparently. They might still be in the COG centers, but they're looking to move out—establish regional centers, move on from all that's happened."

"And we're to be one of those regional centers." Tanda wondered if maybe she was more injured than Miles had let on. Her thoughts felt fuzzy. Or maybe it was the lack of sleep, lack of food, too much adrenaline, mixed with a little snake venom. "What does that mean, exactly? And do we have an option?"

"Honestly, we didn't get that far into it. Current events took precedence."

An armed guard who couldn't have been twenty years old took up position on the other side of the stall door. When he arrived, he opened the stall's door, reminded them not to try anything, then slammed the door shut. He looked like a kid to Tanda. How had he managed to get caught up in this?

As the day wore on and the sun rose higher, the barn grew warmer. It didn't matter. Somehow they slept. Then woke. Drank from an old bucket filled with dirty rainwater. Miles had doctored Keme's left eye the best he could, but it had swollen completely shut. And her ankle was now swollen twice its normal size. Miles checked it periodically and seemed satisfied that the swelling hadn't expanded up her leg.

They didn't dare speak of plans or strategy. The kid sitting outside the stall's door was listening and would report anything he heard. As the sun made its way toward the west, as the deadline approached, their desperation grew. Miles had picked up a small rock. Too small for a weapon, but just right for a writing utensil.

Last Stand!

Both Keme and Tanda nodded.

It was what she would do, what the Council in Alpine would do. It was what she'd tried to convey to Miles and Gonzo and Emmanuel and apparently, that had worked. They'd planned the last-ditch strategy long ago, after the battle with Marfa. Shelter the young and old outside of town. Arm everyone else. Make their stand. What she knew they wouldn't do was hand all of their supplies over to Peyton Steele.

Keme held out his hand for the rock, and Miles dropped it in his palm.

Gus—Supplies?

Miles wrote a single word.

Some

Tanda accepted the rock.

Ammo?

It was their weak point, a fact that kept her awake many nights. Without any ammunition, they were basically Neanderthals throwing rocks at one another.

Miles underlined his last word.

Some was better than none.

# of men?

He hesitated, as if he were counting in his head, then wrote

14

Well. That was a disappointment. They'd sent 14 men to set up a regional center? It suggested the US government was running a bit thin. How many people had fit inside their COG centers? How many had survived the year underground?

That worry was offset by another thought. It was increasingly obvious to her that Steele's group was operating on its own. Otherwise, their supplies wouldn't be so desperately low. It explained why they were so eager to put their hands on what Alpine had.

Gus Martinez offered something she hadn't thought possible. She'd stopped looking for it, even when they'd activated Thornfield's beacon. She hadn't believed the billionaire would come, and when he did fly into town, she hadn't believed he would offer to help them.

Was Gus Martinez different? Was he there to help the people of Alpine or simply take from them?

As to whether they should accept whatever deal this regional task force was operating, she couldn't say. She couldn't even seriously consider such a thing.

It wouldn't matter if they didn't stop Steele.

Miles once again took the rock and scrubbed out what they'd written in the dirt.

Make our move in Alpine. Not b4.

Tanda didn't like it. She didn't want Steele to ever set foot in their town again. But she also couldn't stop him. Not here, bound, disarmed. Not surrounded by his men. As decrepit a group as they made, they easily numbered a dozen.

With three against twelve, they didn't stand a chance. Not when one of them couldn't see out of one eye. One couldn't walk well. And she and Keme hadn't eaten in twenty-four hours. Trying a counterattack now made no sense.

So she nodded.

Keme rested his head back against the wall. At least the bleeding had stopped, but her brother looked spent. Spent and also a little feral. Something in his good eye gave her pause. Even now when he looked at her, he offered one long solemn look before he shut it again... and something told her that Keme had crossed a line mentally and emotionally. She wasn't actually sure what her brother would do, but she did know that it would be directed at Peyton Steele and it would be merciless.

After another hour, Miles moved to unwrap her right ankle.

She wanted to bat him away. Wanted to insist she was fine, but the rattlesnake bite had terrified her. Though there was nothing he could do, having him look at it lessened the terror that threatened to consume her. Tanda didn't want to die. She wanted to go back to Alpine and live out her years with Logan in the town she loved with the people who had become her family. But if she were going to die, she'd damn sure take Steele out before that happened.

When Miles had completely unwrapped her leg, they both stared at it. She knew the swelling had come down because she could now see her ankle. What was left was some discoloration and two fang marks. Miles looked at her, wriggled his eyebrows, and smiled. Then he picked up the rock and wrote a single word.

Lucky

Yeah. Right.

Try walking?

She nodded. Miles helped her stand, and she, at first gingerly, then with more confidence, put her weight on her right foot and walked the length of the stall. It wasn't good as new. She had a pronounced limp, and she might not be able to run. But she could stand. She could fight.

As Miles helped lower her back to the ground, she caught Keme staring at her. She gave him a thumbs up. He almost smiled.

Thirty minutes later, one of Peyton's guys threw their shoes over the stall door. "Time to go, kids. You're going to want to put those on."

Tanda had been wearing an old pair of high-topped sneakers rather than her hiking boots. The hiking boot would have protected her from a random snake bite. Wouldn't have helped much with what happened a few hours earlier. Even with the shoe that barely covered her ankle, she didn't think she could put it on. The swelling hadn't abated enough for that. She thought she'd have to ride with one bare foot, but Miles took one side of the shoe, Keme took the other, and they pulled the fabric apart, splitting it along the seam.

"You're going to want new ones when we get home," Miles said. Then he untied the laces, guided the shoe over her foot, and tied the laces loosely around the shoe so it wouldn't fall off her foot.

They were prodded out of the stall by the same kid with the same stupid .22 rifle. Tanda was sorely tempted to grab it from him and give him a thrashing with the thing. She didn't because there were six other men, all armed, waiting for them.

"Got your horses all ready for you," Peyton said, a smile spreading across his face.

Tanda's temper again threatened to boil over. "Where are the saddles?"

"Saddles? I don't remember that you rode in with saddles."

"We'll be back for those," Tanda said. "While your dead body is lying lifeless in Alpine."

"Big talk for someone who can't mount a horse."

It was true. She couldn't stand on her right foot well enough to throw her left over. And she couldn't throw her right over because it was still tingly and numb. Then Keme and Miles were on either side of her, boosting her up, even though their wrists were still bound. Keme had no trouble mounting his horse, even with one bad eye. Miles took a deep breath and tried to imitate what Keme had done, but his horse was spooked and it still took three tries.

The assholes surrounding them had a good laugh over that one.

Steele had at least left the bridles on the horses. Tanda tried to feel grateful that they wouldn't have to ride hanging on to the horses' manes. She ought to be relieved they hadn't decided to eat one of the mares. No doubt it was because they were picturing an old-fashioned buffet of food once they raided Alpine's supplies.

"Don't try anything funny, now," Steele said. "Dusty here's a good shot. So am I. You remember that, right? I won't hesitate, Tanda. I was the person who shot your hippy friend and the other guy who looked like he ought to be wearing a suit."

"Like ducks in a barrel," Dusty said.

Maybe she'd kill Dusty first. Let Steele watch and worry.

Bold thoughts for a woman riding bareback, unarmed, hands tied, with one foot still swollen from a damn snakebite.

Bold, but not entirely out of the question.

Keme shot her a warning glance that as plainly as the spoken word said *wait*.

They rode in silence back toward their home.

The sun kissed the horizon as they entered Alpine, passed Sul Ross University, and encountered no one.

CHAPTER 15

Gus was not a soldier. Even after a year of living among soldiers, he understood that there was a basic difference between himself and the men and women on his team. They had each taken a vow to protect America—its institutions, its government, its people. He would do the same, but he didn't have the skills or training that they had, despite Aimee's attempt to make sure he could point a gun and shoot accurately.

"They've passed Sul Ross." Dixie's voice came over the radio—containing a calmness that said there was nothing to worry about. Just another day in America.

The fact that their radios still worked was one reason the needle had moved toward success in Gus's analysis. They had superior training, better weapons, some technology, and the element of surprise. Steele was not expecting them. He knew nothing about them. Gus would bet his reputation on it. Hell, he was betting their lives on it.

"Wait for my order," Aimee said.

The echo of horse hooves reached them. He had the

random thought that a deserted town had a different sound to it—a silence so filled with loss and tragedy and times past that it pressed down on you like the weight of a thousand blankets.

DIXIE WATCHED the last of Steele's group proceed south of the Sul Ross Campus. Twelve people in all—Steele, six additional men and two women, plus the three from Alpine. Tanda, Miles, and Keme had been placed in the middle of the group so she hadn't been able to see them well. For some reason, they rode bareback and Tanda's right foot seemed to stick out at an odd angle.

She was about to call it—about to initiate the maneuver that would close off any retreat by Steele's men when Liam's voice came over the radio.

"There are two more holding back, half a mile north of the campus."

That would be near the McCoy's Building Supply.

"I'll meet you there."

"Move fast. Approach from the north."

TANDA WASN'T SURPRISED that Alpine was deserted, or at least it seemed to be. She was actually proud. They'd followed the plan. They'd initiated *Last Stand*. A small part of her relaxed– the part that had been worried about the children and the elderly and the sick. With that minute relaxation, she could focus on the battle about to take place.

Her senses sharpened.

She glimpsed the back of someone dashing into the shadows of a cross street, heard the sound of horse hooves and the occasional soft thump of a boot against pavement. Part of the Alpine group was behind them, but they weren't coming closer. They weren't advancing yet on Steele's group, which meant someone—probably Liam—had spotted Steele's people who had split off from the main group.

The sound faded away.

Steele didn't seem to notice any of it because Peyton Steele was completely focused on the prize ahead of him, the supplies stacked in the center of the street.

She expected Dixie or Ron or maybe even Logan to step out in front of the boxes and crates. Or maybe no one. Maybe the supplies were merely a diversion, and they were waiting for Peyton and his lackeys to step into the trap. Neither of those things happened. Instead someone that Tanda didn't know, someone she'd never even met, stepped out into the middle of the street.

He wasn't from Alpine.

And he didn't look like a soldier.

But she had seen him before—riding between Dixie and Liam.

When Aimee had nodded his direction, Gus walked to the middle of Main Street. They hadn't known how many people Steele would have with him. The group moving toward him was both larger than they'd hoped and smaller than they'd feared. Four in the front, including Steele. Two on each side. Possibly three more in the back, and in the middle rode the three people that this town was determined to protect.

The guy on the right had to be Miles Turner, the doctor who had lived on Old Ranch Road. The man who had suffered the tragic loss of his family well before the satellites fell.

There was no doubt that the man on the left was Keme—tall, definitely a mix of Hispanic and Kiowa, with a busted-up face and an unreadable expression.

And in the middle was Tanda. Dixie had tried to describe her friend. Tried and failed. Tanda Lopez was smaller than he'd expected, and she rode with her right foot sticking out awkwardly, but it was the expression on her face that would have caused Gus to know her anywhere. Fierce. Unrelenting. Almost stoic.

Gus stepped in front of the large stash of empty boxes and crates they'd set in the middle of the road. Some had *Meal, Ready-to-Eat* stamped on the side. The crates were filled with empty canning jars, although there had been some dissension about that. Canning jars were an important resource, and no one was making new ones. They would need them for storing the harvest from their gardens.

"Don't shoot the canning jars," an older woman named Peggy Looper had emphasized. "A bullet can kill, but so can starvation."

Steele's group wouldn't get close enough to figure out the stash was a ruse, and Gus was confident any firefight would be aimed toward people, not supplies.

Steele held up his hand and the party came to a stop.

If Keme and Tanda were surprised to see a person they didn't know representing Alpine, they certainly didn't show it. Perhaps Miles had managed to catch them up on Gus's group. For whatever reason, they showed no outward reaction to his appearance. Gus couldn't actually read their expressions. These three were focused. They were in the zone. They were ready.

"My name's Gus—Gus Martinez. We have what you asked for."

"Smart. I think I like you, Martinez." Steele said it by elongating the first two syllables and placing extra emphasis on the last. Mar-tee—NEZ.

This guy was really a prick.

He ogled the boxes. "Are you sure that's all of it?"

For his answer, Gus spread out his hands. As if to say, *search me if you'd like.*

"If you're keeping what is now rightfully ours, we'll be back."

Gus nodded, still not wasting any breath or energy by trying to reason with this guy. Why would he? There was absolutely no chance Peyton Steele would listen to anything Gus had to say.

Keme was staring at the red handkerchief tied around Gus's neck. Staring at it as if he understood. He moved his horse back a step, then two, and to the left. If Gus hadn't been watching him, he wouldn't have noticed, but he was definitely closer to Tanda. Steele hadn't seen the move. Steele's gaze was fixed on the food. When he raised his right hand and flicked his index finger, two of his people rode forward.

Closer.

Closer still.

When their eyes widened—perhaps they noticed the canning jars were empty, he'd never know—Gus pulled his weapon and shot the man on Steele's right. He turned to his left, knowing that Aimee would take care of Steele, but he never got the shot off.

Because that was the moment that hell literally broke loose.

TANDA DIDN'T REALIZE Keme had loosened the ropes around his hands until she felt her brother slap her mare's rump. Roxie bolted, causing Steele's horse to rear up. Keme had seen something that she hadn't and was making sure that she wasn't caught in the middle of it. Roxie galloped through the chaotic melee, and Tanda, somehow, managed to hang on.

The mare was headed for a side street.

Tanda pulled on the reins, turned her horse around, and charged back into the battle—ignoring the pain that shot through her ankle, ignoring the fact that her hands were still tied, ignoring everything except the men and women she meant to kill.

She didn't think of the danger of it. Didn't wonder how she'd fight without a weapon. She wasn't actually aware of making the decision to throw herself into the fray. She was acutely aware of Alpine, of the way the last of the dying light reflected off the windows, of her brothers and sisters around her on all sides, of this threat in their midst. She was aware of the family they had become and her need to protect those fighting as well as those hidden.

Her breathing slowed.

Her mind cleared.

She picked out a target and spurred Roxie toward him.

Dixie and Liam were no longer worried about stealth. The sound of gunfire echoed through the empty streets of Alpine. They galloped north of the parking area where Liam had spotted the two men.

Men.

They were barely that. Seventeen? Maybe eighteen?

As they charged into the parking lot, guns drawn, the two waiting there turned toward them.

Dixie hesitated even though they, too, had raised their guns.

Kids. Certainly not men.

Their shots went wide. Perhaps they'd fired too soon, or maybe they'd never been properly trained. With her peripheral vision, she saw Liam lay chase to the kid on the right who had spurred his horse then headed in the wrong direction—pointed his mount toward an enclosed work area behind the lumber store. He didn't stand a chance against Liam Contreras.

Which left Dixie to deal with the remaining teenager.

The sound of a bullet whizzing by her ear was all Dixie needed to resolve any qualms she might have had about using her weapon. She slowed her horse, took aim, and hit the guy who was now trying to turn his horse and speed away in the opposite direction, no doubt fleeing the double report of a gun coming from the direction his buddy had gone.

"Drop your weapon," Dixie said.

He dropped to the ground, stumbled, fell, then hopped back up to his feet, clutching his left arm. Dixie might have shown mercy then, in spite of what Gus had told them.

This guy was just a kid.

Didn't look as if he needed to shave yet.

He should have been picking out what college to attend or deciding to pursue a vocation. Instead, he raised his gun and aimed it at her once more.

She fired twice.

This time he didn't get up.

Gus's adrenaline spiked as he turned from the man he'd shot, a man who was now bleeding out on the ground.

The scene in the middle of Alpine had turned chaotic.

Tanda's horse had galloped down a side street, but she'd managed to calm it, turn it, and rejoin the fight in the amount of time it took Gus to turn away from the man he'd shot and toward the main group.

Keme slid off his horse and came up behind the man Gus had shot. As the man attempted to raise his handgun, Keme placed his left arm around the man's neck, and with his right, he snapped the man's neck, then snatched up his gun and sprinted into the midst of the fighting. Miles had pivoted his horse and was spurring into Steele's men who were positioned at the back. They weren't accomplished riders. Miles plainly was. Steele's group was outmatched in every way.

Gus watched it all as if in slow motion.

His ears were still ringing from the shot he'd taken. Muzzle flashes sparked in every direction. The distinct smell of gunpowder filled the air. He looked down, saw his gun still in his hand, and took aim as one of Steele's men attempted to charge over him. The man fell from the saddle as the horse turned at the last second and bolted from the center of town.

The two men that had been on Gus's left fled, pulling on their reins and then spurring the horses down a side street. The sound of gunshots rang out from that direction, from north of town, all around him.

Keme was fighting off two of Steele's men who were attempting to drag him back toward one of the adjacent buildings, attempting to use him as a shield. Gus raised his gun, tried to get a clear shot, and waited. He was afraid he'd shoot Keme. Afraid he'd do more harm than good.

Then, as he watched, first one man went down and then the other. Sorrell's work, no doubt about it. He'd positioned himself on top of the train depot with the sniper rifle. Keme didn't hesitate. He'd fallen with the men as they'd died, but now he pushed their bodies away, snatched up both guns, and threw himself back into the gunfight.

Tanda had dismounted her mare and was attempting to run down one of Steele's men. When her ankle gave way, she reached across a dead man—her hands still bound with a rope, pulled his weapon, took aim, and fired. The guy she was chasing dropped in his tracks.

"Shouldn't have tried to run," Gus whispered.

"You're not wrong." He felt Steele's grip around his throat, the pressure of his gun muzzle against his neck.

Why wasn't he dead?

How had he managed to escape Sorrell's aim?

"Nice and slow. I suspect you're important to them if you're the spokesman. No doubt, as important as Tanda Lopez."

"You'd be wrong about that." Gus dropped his head as Aimee had taught him, trying with all of his might to push his chin into his chest which was impossible because Steele's arm was still locked around his neck.

And still, Sorrell took the shot.

The pressure around Gus's neck released instantly.

Then he heard a thud when Steele's body hit the ground.

Superior training. Superior equipment. Even if they'd understood they didn't stand a chance, Steele's group of outlaws wouldn't have given in. Gus knew that as surely as he knew that while the nature of their lives had changed, the nature of man hadn't. Some would always choose the dark path.

Not all.

Maybe not even the majority.

He heard shots coming from the south, the west, the east, and finally the north. Aimee's pincer move. He glanced at his watch. Twenty-two minutes.

Decisive.

Brutal.

Dixie and Liam spurred their horses back toward town. They arrived in time to see the Alpine people mopping up the few stragglers who had made it back through town and were attempting to escape.

She watched Tanda's niece move into an isosceles stance, take aim, and drop one of Steele's men. She didn't smile. Didn't celebrate. Simply holstered the weapon and jogged forward, made sure the man was no longer a threat, removed his gun from his hand and tucked it into her belt.

Someone else went down to their right.

Liam walked his horse up to hers, and they sat there, in the middle of Alpine as the light faded from the day.

The sound of gunfire slowed, then ceased completely.

They'd won.

They'd stood their ground.

Gus turned at the sound of someone coming toward him— Tanda, with Miles on one side and Keme on the other. Miles looked exhausted, but not injured. Tanda was limping badly. Keme had blood running down his arm. He'd found a knife in the melee and tucked it in his waistband. Now he touched his sister's shoulder, they both stopped, and he smiled as he cut the rope binding her hands.

Gus stood there, the air quickly cooling as the day gave way to night. He stood there in the middle of downtown Alpine, Texas. So many miles from his home—or what he'd pretended was home. So many miles from the man he'd once been.

He stepped forward and shook Tanda's hand.

Then Miles's.

Then Keme's.

All three had ridden into town not knowing for certain that the town would fight, but trusting that they would stand true. In spite of what they'd been through, in spite of the dead around them, they stood tall, appeared calm.

"My name's Gus. Gus Martinez. And I work for the US Government."

CHAPTER 16

Dixie felt as if she were walking through her worst nightmare—the smell of gunfire hung in the air, darkness was settling, Alpine was eerily quiet. The shooting had stopped. The attacking group who would have left the people of Alpine defenseless and hungry—had been stopped. No one was doing a victory dance, though. The taking of another life wasn't something to celebrate.

It took less than an hour to stack the bodies on the back of a flatbed. One of Aimee's G-wagens would pull the trailer to the outskirts of town where they'd be buried. Liam had left to ride patrol—which had been doubled just in case there were any stragglers. Dixie made her way back to the middle of the town. She needed to see Tanda and Miles and Keme with her own eyes.

"What happened to your foot?"

"Snakebite."

Logan was unwrapping her ankle, applying a clean compress, checking her pupils and her blood pressure.

"I'm fine." She batted his hand away, but he grabbed it, squeezed, leaned forward, and kissed her.

Tanda shook her head as if to say *what am I going to do with this guy?* Then she stood and embraced Dixie.

"You drew the short straw." Dixie hadn't realized until that moment that she felt guilty about that. It could have been she and Liam who were taken captive. It could have gone the other way.

"You brought back reinforcement." Tanda nodded toward Gus, who was meeting with his team. "He seems like one of the good guys."

"I think so." Dixie was grateful for the darkness, glad that her friend couldn't see the slow blush she'd never been able to control.

"There's something in your voice that tells me there's more. Promise to catch me up tomorrow?"

"Promise."

Aisha was attempting to get a good look at Keme's eye. As usual, he wasn't the most cooperative patient. One bark from Caleb, though, and he settled down.

"You're going to have to teach me that," Aisha called out to the other doctor.

"Stick around here long enough, and you'll develop a style of your own."

"It's possible we have too many doctors in this town," Keme grumbled.

"Doubtful." Aisha nodded at Dixie as she approached. "Is he always like this?"

"Pretty much."

"Thanks for selling me out, Peters."

"Anytime, man. Anytime." She squeezed his arm, then went in search of Miles.

She found him handing out water and the few rations

they'd left in town—giving water and energy bars to the people who had fought and defended Alpine. He looked ready to literally drop to the ground.

"I got this," she said.

He started to argue with her, thought better of it, and managed a heartfelt, "Thanks."

Dixie realized that this town, these people, had become her family. They knew each other so well that she knew Miles would set down a bowl of water for Zeus before getting anything for himself. Keme would not do what Aisha was suggesting as far as taking it easy, but he would leave something at her doorstep in thanks for her attention—wildflowers, an aloe vera plant, maybe a jar of canned food from his mother. That was the kind of guy Keme was. And Tanda would remain in the downtown area, with Logan at her side until she finally relented and walked away, climbed the hill to Sul Ross, and crawled into bed. Tanda would be the last to leave.

Dixie understood that she didn't know Gustavo Martinez, not really. You couldn't actually know a person in a few days. You couldn't become acquainted with their habits or nature that quickly, or know the things that they cherished. But Dixie realized in that moment that she did want to know all of those things about Gus. Hopefully he would stick around long enough for her to do so.

The next morning, two of Aimee's people took a G-wagen north to the Gutterson Ranch, retrieved the stolen saddles, and confirmed there was no one at the old survivalist's place.

"Didn't find the old man's body," Aimee reported to the Council the following evening.

"Gutterson might have escaped into the desert," Keme said.

He was now able to see out of his left eye, but the bruising had turned an ugly mottle of purple and dark green. He'd also been grazed by a bullet during the brief battle, and the biceps of his right arm were wrapped with what looked like a sheet that had been torn into strips. The sheet had been a light floral pattern. It looked so incongruous wrapped around his gunshot wound. The wolfish grin he tossed Dixie's way caused her to smile. How could she not? Keme Lopez would do anything to protect his sister, his friends, this town. Keme was the best of what had come out of June 6th.

"Gutterson was a tough old guy," Keme said. "He would have known he couldn't survive against a dozen outlaws. He may show up yet."

"What's next?" Tanda asked. She wasn't one to tiptoe around a thing. She sat between Logan and Keme, her gaze locked on Aimee.

For her answer, Aimee simply nodded toward Gus.

And Gus, well, Gus smiled at Dixie before he answered Tanda's question. Dixie's heart did a bounce. Impossible. Hearts didn't bounce. Or did they? She'd never fallen in love as a teenager. Even what she had with Hunter was more akin to an amazing friendship than this. This? This was frightening. The depth of her feelings for this man she barely knew was startling in its intensity. Downright terrifying.

Still, she smiled back.

"I haven't briefed Colonel Webb yet, who will in turn brief General Kendricks."

"Some things about the military never change." Liam was smiling as he said it.

"Our comms are down. Not unusual. They work an average of once a week, owing to satellite positions, etc. The global network communication system we once had isn't functioning —yet. We are still able to get a message through though sometimes it takes a few days."

"But you will brief them." Tanda very obviously felt

conflicted about contacting the government. She'd lost her trust in the powers that were supposed to protect them. They all had.

"Yes. I will."

"What can you tell us about their future plans for the regional centers?" Tanda didn't look away. Didn't pretend that she wasn't challenging him. "What are their future plans for Alpine?"

"There won't be martial law, which I've heard is a big concern. In all likelihood, you won't see much immediate change."

Miles held out a hand, palm facing the floor, and wiggled it back and forth. Everyone laughed. It was their signal for a draw—not great, not terrible, often the best they could hope for.

"I can tell you what I'll recommend," Gus went on. "Alpine should be one of the regional centers. You have a solid group of people. There's enough land to cultivate and enough wildlife to support a medium-sized community. You're also remote enough that you're easy to defend from groups of urban survivors who might want what you have."

"We've been defending ourselves for over a year," Keme pointed out.

"You have, and you've done a good job. But when people hear Uncle Sam is in the area, I suspect you'll see an influx of folks—both good and bad."

"I wouldn't mind regaining some of our population," Harper said. "A town needs people—we could use more farmers, teachers, doctors, even writers."

"Based on the information I received before leaving Raven Rock, the government's hope is to deploy larger teams by winter, perhaps even in the fall." He hesitated, then added, "I wouldn't expect help for the remaining months of summer."

"We have a trade route," Logan said. "Folks who bring food up from the Rio Grande Valley. We trade them deer meat, salt, whatever they need that we have an excess of. And we've had rains. We've done this before. We know how to survive a summer surrounded by the Chihuahuan desert with nothing to depend on but ourselves."

"We have done it before," Tanda said. "And we'll do it again."

"If you don't have any other questions for me..." Gus waited a moment, giving anyone who wanted to speak a chance. No one did, so he continued. "If you don't mind, I have a few questions."

Tanda sat back and shrugged.

Dixie tried to repress a smile. Maybe it was the fact that they'd faced a renegade force and won—again. Maybe it was that things were back to their new normal. Whatever the reason, she felt almost giddy with relief. And though she was a person who usually loathed meetings, she was enjoying this one.

"You saw my bandana." Gus waited for Keme to nod in the affirmative. "You seemed to know what that meant."

"We saw something similar traveling back from Dallas."

"You went to Dallas?"

"To find my son. To bring him and his family home."

"Okay. I want to know more about that when you have time. But back to the bandanas—"

"Groups used the bandanas to signal they were on the right side of things. In a battle where the opponent doesn't wear uniforms, it was useful. Didn't always work, but it helped. Certainly helped like-minded individuals not get killed by friendly fire."

"You were quick to work that out."

Keme shrugged, apparently having no more to offer, so Gus turned his attention to Tanda.

"The snake bite you suffered, was it intentional?"

"Oh, yeah. They put me in a corral, had a rattler in a cage like you might catch a possum in. Opened the cage and watched the show."

"How did you survive it?"

It was Miles who answered that question. "She's tough."

"But a rattlesnake's venom—"

Tanda held up her hands, palms out, fingers splayed. "My *abuela* taught me a lot of things."

"How to wrestle a rattler?"

"How to confront a problem head-on. In this case, that strategy worked. I did my best to keep my heart rate low. That helped, and then Gutterson's bullet saved my life."

"Why are you asking these things?" Miles didn't sound confrontational, merely curious.

"When I coded my model, my program, I was using what we knew about people and society at the time, before the events of June 6th. I'm beginning to think that may not be entirely accurate."

He'd explained this to Dixie the night before. Long after they should have been sleeping, they sat outside her duplex and dissected the events of the day. They'd talked through the fact that they each felt inherently different than the person they once were. Now he was stretching that theory to include all of Alpine, maybe all of the world.

"You want to know if people have changed—if *we* have changed." Tanda let her gaze drift around the room. "The answer is in front of you, Gus. You might not have known us before, but you knew what a small-town police chief acted like. How a doctor and a fire chief responded to emergencies. You haven't been in Alpine long, but you've seen enough to know that we're not who we were. And we never will be again."

Gus nodded in agreement.

It was Aimee who sat forward and returned to the previous topic. "My team was tasked with bringing Gus to Alpine, setting up a remote base in Fort Davis, and preparing for a transition team."

"What is a transition team?" Dixie asked. "Transition from what? To what?"

"Back *to what*," Gus said. "Hopefully back to the modern world."

"Electricity?" Logan asked.

"Yes, of a sort. Generators, solar panels, portable wind turbines. You won't have air conditioning, but the lights will come back on."

Dixie raised a hand, like a kid in class. "Supplies?"

"The government has more than you'd think, even after a year in hardened facilities. There's plenty of seed—"

"Heirloom?" Harper's voice rose in hope.

"Yes. Someone thought far enough ahead to know that we'd need corn that could produce more corn. Heirloom seeds have been stored in bulk around the country."

"Medical supplies?" This was from Aisha, who would more than likely be taking Gonzo's place on the Council—she'd proven her loyalty to Alpine since moving there. Plus she had a needed perspective that none of them did. She had once set her sights on travelling through space.

"Some. We won't immediately have enough insulin to go around. Stockpiles are also insufficient in regard to vaccines, blood pressure medication, even cancer treatment drugs. But we do have a sufficient amount of antibiotics, antimalarials, pain relievers, etc."

"How is that possible?" Tanda asked. "The government quite obviously was not prepared to save the American people, though it will be a long time before people forget that they were able to save themselves."

"Would you rather there be no continuity of government?"

"I didn't say that. But make no mistake, it will be a sticking point."

"Understood."

"Back to my original question. How is it possible that they would have enough power infrastructure, farming supplies, and basic medical supplies for all America?"

"To put it bluntly, America is much smaller than it used to be. We don't have exact numbers for today, but before June 6th there were approximately three hundred and forty million people across these United States. That number? We're not even close to it now. The reason there is enough is a direct result of that decrease in numbers." When the Alpine people looked at each other skeptically, Gus pushed the point. "How many people lived in Alpine before June 6th?"

Logan took that one. "Six thousand in Alpine. Ten thousand in Brewster County."

"And today?"

Tanda glanced at Miles.

"Eight hundred and twenty-four," he said. "As of last night."

"Fourteen percent." Gus didn't have to do the calculation in his head. He knew the numbers, probably knew them better than the people sitting in the room with him did. "If that statistic holds true for America as a whole—"

"Forty-seven point six." Aisha sighed and sat back. "Our national population, more than likely, has dropped from 340 million to 47.6 million. That's how we'll have enough."

As the meeting broke up, Dixie held back. She and Gus walked out into the night together and down to the parking area. He'd be leaving in one of the G-Wagens for Fort Davis. She'd be walking to her little duplex on the other side of Alpine.

He pulled her close and kissed her softly. "Want me to walk you home?"

"I think I'm good."

"I do love an independent woman."

"Good thing since I'm pretty sure that's all we have left."

"You're a special person. You know that, right? If we hadn't had your backing, if you hadn't stood up for us before the Council, yesterday's attack might have gone differently."

"I hear what you're saying, but I don't think it was dependent on me. Any idea of politics fled in the days and weeks following June 6th. The Council would have agreed to accept your help regardless of their opinion of you, because the Council's sole purpose is to facilitate the survival of Alpine." She glanced over at the waiting G-wagen. "Will you stay?"

"Stay?"

"After the reinforcements arrive."

"Yeah. I'm staying."

"And if they order you not to?"

"You forget. I'm a contractor to the government. I'm a sociologist. I can quit anytime."

"Always thought we could use a sociologist in Alpine."

"Did you?"

To which she simply kissed him again, then turned and walked away.

～

Tanda sat next to Logan, their backs against the Sul Ross University sign, their eyes on the stars. Logan reached for her hand, squeezed it, then said, "Penny for your thoughts."

"Do you have a penny?"

"I could probably find one."

She shook her head, hopped somewhat clumsily to her feet, paced a few feet away and stood there a minute, then two. Her back to Logan. Her face to the unknown. But that was wrong, she realized. The future had always been unknown. They'd simply been foolish enough, back in the days of yore, back before June 6th, to pretend it was knowable.

She turned, walked back, and sat beside him, close enough that they were sitting hip to hip. "It's hard to imagine."

"A modern Alpine?"

"Everything. All of it. The lights coming back on. Having enough food and medicine. Having help with the defense of Alpine. Returning to what my job was—being the police chief of our town. Instead of... " Her words faded into silence. How could she explain what she'd endured and the things she'd done?

Fortunately, she didn't have to. She only had to explain what they were willing to do. "Instead of the defender of Alpine. I suppose those of us who have stayed, those of us who have survived, will always have a little of the defender in us."

"Yup. It won't happen overnight," he reminded her.

"May not happen at all." Did she wish that? More modern was better. If they could avoid the traps of the modern age, the unchecked dependence on technology, the inability to plan for worst-case scenarios, the arrogance. "I think that what happened... I don't mean the satellites falling. I'm talking about our complete lack of planning for such an event. I think it was caused by a lack of imagination."

"Explain it to me."

She turned toward him, "We thought we'd outsmarted nature."

"The Kessler Effect wasn't a result of nature."

"Or maybe it was. We don't really know it if was sparked by an intentional act of war or was the result of an accident."

"Okay. Possibly it was a result of our inability to understand the laws of nature, physics, objects in motion."

"We thought we did though."

"So it comes back to..."

"Imagination." They said the word in the same breath, softly, trying it out to see if it fit.

"We were so confident. We couldn't imagine anything going wrong. Anything knocking us off our technological pedestal."

"Tower of Babel."

"Yup."

They were silent for another moment.

"And now, Police Chief Lopez, the question is this. Have we learned anything from the last year? I don't mean you and I or the people of Alpine. I mean has the world learned anything? Have the tech geniuses and the politicians?"

"Time will tell, I guess." She thought about that, and as she did, her resolve grew until she had to voice her promise to someone. She could start with the guy she loved. So she turned to Logan, though she couldn't make out his features in the darkness. "It's a good hope—that things might improve before winter. That the lights might come back on and with them a whole slew of supplies could be delivered. I want to believe that. But whether those things happen or not, I won't forget. I won't let Alpine forget. We will never be that vulnerable again."

Logan put his arm around her, pulled her in close until

there was nothing between the two of them. "Gotcha. I'll keep my doctoring skills up to date, even if I'm able to go back to only treating animals."

"That's all a girl could ask for."

"Asked and answered."

CHAPTER 17

Gus stepped out of the Fort Davis National Park's headquarters building into a Texas sky resplendent with stars. It exceeded anything he could have imagined. The Milky Way was something he'd never seen before. The lights of DC had obscured the stars for most of his adult life, and then he'd spent a year underground. He breathed in the fresh air. Felt a coolness as the heat of the day fled. Heard the sounds of horses in the corral, night birds, the howl of a coyote.

No traffic.

No cry of an ambulance or beep of a car alarm.

No generator pushing recirculated air through the vents.

Just the desert and the night and distant sounds of a few good men and women.

Aimee walked across the parade ground, past the flag pole that now held the stars and stripes each day. She stopped next to him, turned around, and surveyed Fort Davis. "This place has made a good base."

"It has."

"Guess that's why they built it, all those years ago." She paused a moment, and then asked, "You spoke with the colonel?"

"I did."

"Don't leave me hanging here, Martinez."

"They still haven't heard from the Oregon group, but all the other teams have called in. The Chicago group has been deemed a complete loss. The Georgia group returned to Raven Rock. So, including us, that makes nine teams still deployed and accounted for."

"And what the other teams, the surviving teams encountered... Did it match your model?"

"In many ways, yes. We predicted the chaos, the destruction, even the fact that some groups positioned in the right place, with the right set of skills, and in an environment that could support life would survive."

"But—"

He scrubbed a hand over his face. "We didn't predict how independent people would become. Two groups flat-out refused help. Vowed to fight to the death should the government attempt to intrude, and one group actually did that, killing every man and woman in the Chicago team."

"Hard to imagine."

"Exactly."

"So one hasn't reported in, two answered with a flat no—one violently, the other definitively. What about the other nine?"

"The other eight are a go. Still waiting to hear from Oregon."

"Best case, seventy-five percent." She shrugged. "I'd call that a win."

"Deployment of assets and supplies will begin immediately, but the regional centers closest to COG facilities will be the first in line."

"Not Alpine."

"Not Alpine."

"Winter?"

"I hope so. I hope supplies and reinforcements arrive before the cold hits. According to Dixie, last winter was awfully hard on these people." He hesitated and then added, "But it might be spring."

"And what are we to do until then?"

"Stay. Watch. Help if we can. I'll continue working on the model."

"Model for—"

"The reestablishment of these United States."

"Has a nice ring to it."

"Yes, it does."

She started to turn away with a "Goodnight then," but he stopped her.

"When reinforcements do arrive, your people will be given the option of staying or being deployed elsewhere."

Aimee nodded, or he thought she did. It was a little hard to tell in the dark.

"Given my choice of assignments, I'd aim farther west. No offense."

"None taken. Do you have people that direction?"

"I did."

It sat between them for a heartbeat, then two.

"Can't know if they're still alive," she said. "But I'd like to check on them."

"Would you have gone into Raven Rock if you'd known?"

"Yes." No hesitation.

Just when the sociologist in Gus thought he understood a person, they surprised him. This softer side of Aimee, this human side, surprised him. He'd thought she was all Kevlar vests and gun sights. "Why?"

"It's what we do, Gus. When you join the military, you take an oath. Support and defend the Constitution. Obey the orders of the president. Obey your commanding officers."

"Not every enlisted person did that."

"If they had, things might have gone very differently."

"Plenty of blame to spread around."

"I suppose."

They were silent a moment. The sounds of the Texas night seemed to swell—tree frogs, crickets, birds, the wind—then recede.

She asked, "What about you?"

"I'll stay."

"You like it here."

"A hell of a lot better than DC or Raven Rock. And I don't have any people. Didn't have any before June 6th." It was true, but they both knew that part of the reason he was staying was Dixie Peters.

Did he have enough faith in these people, the government's plan, and his model to build a life here? As quickly as the thought entered his mind it was followed by *gotta build one somewhere.*

Aimee wished him a good night and headed off in the direction of the sleeping quarters. Gus sat on the wooden step of what was left of the main headquarters of Fort Davis, built and commissioned one hundred and seventy years earlier. He stared toward Alpine, though he couldn't see it. There were no lights in the distance, except for starlight.

What he hadn't shared with Aimee was the colonel's belief that the United States of America would be attacked by foreign forces before the nine regional centers were up and running.

"A wounded animal is a vulnerable one," Webb had said.

"While we're setting up the regional centers, we'll also be preparing for war."

Maybe that would happen.

Maybe it wouldn't.

What Gus knew, without the smallest bit of doubt, was that the people in Alpine would be prepared for whatever came next. They were prepared before he'd even arrived.

The End

Love the Kessler Effect Series? Sign up to receive my newsletter and be the first to know about the last book in this series, *Veil of Light*, releasing in 2025.

Also receive a **FREE BOOK** when you join my mailing list. Plus, get updates on new releases, deals, and more from Vannetta Chapman. Visit my webpage to sign up.

www.VannettaChapman.com

Already a subscriber? Provide your email again so we can send you the FREE book if you haven't received it previously. You will also continue to receive exclusive offers in your inbox.

THANK YOU FOR READING, *Veil of Hope.* I hope you enjoyed the story. If you did, please consider rating the book or leaving a review at at the book retailer of your choice.

AUTHOR'S NOTE

This book is dedicated to the firefighting crews of Alpine, Texas. As I began writing this book, the state of Texas was inundated with terrific storms—high winds, hail, and tornadoes that rolled over the state in one wave after another. While much of the state dealt with flooding, Alpine remained somewhat dry. Then, on Sunday afternoon, May 26th, a fire broke out in the business section, leaving five businesses in ruins. Volunteer firefighters from Alpine, Marathon, Terlingua, Marfa, Jeff Davis County, and the Texas A&M Forest Service assisted. On Wednesday, in the nearby town of Marathon, officials deployed snow plows after a 50-degree temperature swing and two feet of hail. Such is life in this rugged part of Texas. To say these people are tough would be an understatement.

I visited and thoroughly researched Alpine, Texas and the surrounding locations mentioned in this book. Any changes made within the pages of this book were done so in order to expedite the plot of the book.

In 1978, NASA scientist Donald J. Kessler published a paper

titled, "Collision Frequency of Artificial Satellites: The Creation of a Debris Belt." This paper described a cascading collision of lower orbital satellites, something that has since been termed the Kessler Effect or the Kessler Syndrome. I have done my best to adequately present his theories within the text of this story. Any errors made in that representation are my own.

Many people were helpful in the writing of this book, including Kristy Kreymer, Tracy Luscombe, and Teresa Lynn.

And, of course, Bob—I love you, babe.

ALSO BY VANNETTA CHAPMAN

DEFENDING AMERICA SERIES
Coyote's Revenge (Book 1)
Roswell's Secret (Book 2)

KESSLER EFFECT SERIES
Veil of Mystery (Book 1 - a Prequel)
Veil of Anarchy (Book 2)
Veil of Confusion (Book 3)
Veil of Destruction (Book 4)
Veil of Stillness (Book 5)
Veil of Hope (Book 6)

ALLISON QUINN SERIES
Her Solemn Oath (Book 1 - a Prequel)
Support and Defend (Book 2)
Against All Enemies (Book 3)

STANDALONE NOVEL
Security Breach

FOR A COMPLETE LIST OF MY BOOKS, VISIT MY
Complete Book List

CONTACT THE AUTHOR

Share Your Thoughts With the author:
Your comments will be forwarded to the author when you send
them to vannettachapman@gmail.com.

Submit your review of this book to:
vannettachapman@gmail.com or via the connect/contact
button on the author's website at:
VannettaChapman.com.

Sign up for the author's newsletter at:
VannettaChapman.com.

www.ingramcontent.com/pod-product-compliance
Lightning Source LLC
Chambersburg PA
CBHW020239160726
47987CB00019B/194